CONTACTING THE DEAD
CAN BE DANGEROUS . . .

After a few minutes spent settling in, Simon called the small group to attention.

"We have a specific goal tonight," he said, looking from one face to another. "We will attempt to contact Mariele's deceased husband, whose name is Ben. We have an article of Ben's clothing which we will pass around the table now. As you all know, we have a good chance of getting through to Ben if we all concentrate our energies."

Once the jacket had made the rounds, Simon handed it back to Mariele and took her hand. She noticed that everyone at the table now held hands with the person on either side of them. She expected to hear a lot of mumbo jumbo. But to her surprise, the people at the table fell silent. The only sound she could hear was the sound of Simon's labored breathing.

"We are looking for Ben Hollander," Simon shouted, startling Mariele. "Ben Hollander come forward!" He repeated the same words over and over, and then fell silent.

Mariele had heard the term "pregnant silence," but she hadn't experienced one before. The room was filled with a silence so intense that there seemed to be one layer of silence on top of another.

It was into this vast well of silence that Mariele's dead husband spoke her name.

"Ben! Is that you?"

"Mari . . . it's bad. So close . . . so many. If you knew . . . couldn't live with the horror of it. Help. . . ."

. . . SOMETIMES THEY ANSWER

HAUTALA'S HORROR AND
SUPERNATURAL SUSPENSE

GHOST LIGHT (4320, $4.99)
Alex Harris is searching for his kidnapped children, but only the ghost of their dead mother can save them from his murderous rage.

DARK SILENCE (3923, $5.99)
Dianne Fraser is trying desperately to keep her family—and her own sanity—from being pulled apart by the malevolent forces that haunt the abandoned mill on their property.

COLD WHISPER (3464, $5.95)
Tully can make Sarah's every wish come true, but Sarah lives in teror because Tully doesn't understand that some wishes aren't meant to come true.

LITTLE BROTHERS (4020, $4.50)
The "little brothers" have returned, and this time there will be no escape for the boy who saw them kill his mother.

NIGHT STONE (3681, $4.99)
Their new house was a place of darkness, shadows, long-buried secrets, and a force of unspeakable evil.

MOONBOG (3356, $4.95)
Someone—or something—is killing the children in the little town of Holland, Maine.

MOONDEATH (1844, $3.95)
When the full moon rises in Cooper Falls, a beast driven by bloodlust and savage evil stalks the night.

Available wherever paperbacks are sold, or order direct from the Publisher. Send cover price plus 50¢ per copy for mailing and handling to Penguin USA, P.O. Box 999, c/o Dept. 17109, Bergenfield, NJ 07621. Residents of New York and Tennessee must include sales tax. DO NOT SEND CASH.

graythings

PAT GRAVERSEN

ZEBRA BOOKS
KENSINGTON PUBLISHING CORP.

For my friends at Garden State Horror Writers.
See you in print, guys!

ZEBRA BOOKS are published by

Kensington Publishing Corp.
850 Third Avenue
New York, NY 10022

First Printing: March, 1995

Printed in the United States of America

Dying
Is an art, like everything else.
I do it exceptionally well.

I do it so it feels like hell.
I do it so it feels real.
I guess you could say I've a call.

—Sylvia Plath, from "Lady Lazarus"

And to die is different from what anyone supposed . . .

—Walt Whitman, from *Song of Myself*

prologue

She heard the other mourners whispering behind her, but the meaning of their words stopped just short of reaching her. She caught snatches of their gossip, blown on the wind that tousled her shoulder-length blond hair. Did it matter to her what they said? Did she care that they thought she looked pale and drawn, that the plain black dress made her appear to be even thinner than she really was? If she had applied too much eye makeup or splashed on too much Red, that was her business, wasn't it?

I'm twenty-six years old, she thought bitterly, and the love of my life is dead. My Ben, the only man I ever wanted, is lying in that box, waiting to be lowered into the ground. While I try to go on with my life, his body will rot; maggots will swarm through his putrid flesh. But where will Ben be, the real Ben, who loved me and promised never to leave me?

The real Ben has been gone a long time, came the answer, and she knew that it was the truth. The man she had married two years ago was not the same man who fell asleep behind the wheel and drove his sports car into a wall at high speed. The real Ben had been gone a long, long time.

Ben was dead! The reality had struck her as she tried to get herself together for the funeral. She had been searching every corner of her bedroom for the new black slip she'd purchased recently. She hadn't owned a black slip, and she'd bought this one two weeks ago when she went to Macy's for a new teddy. Was that a premonition? Had some small insistent voice guided her to the display rack and placed the wisp of silk in her hands? Buy this, buy this. Your husband is going to die, buy this.

She stepped forward and looked past the coffin, trying to see into the hole that had been dug at dawn and discreetly covered with a grass-green tarp. Ben had wanted children so badly.

"I'm sorry, Ben," she said aloud, and tongues started wagging again. "I'm sorry," she said louder, daring anyone to try and shut her up. The minister stopped talking and looked at her, then said something she didn't understand.

He approached her and placed a red rose in her hand. When she didn't move, he gave her a little nudge, and she understood that the rose was for Ben, her last tribute. She closed her eyes, and everything turned gray. When she opened them, an errant beam of sunlight sneaked from behind the clouds and glanced off the silver casket.

She felt the earth tremble and give way beneath her. She toppled forward, and the last thing she remembered was the hope that no one would pick her up. Maybe if they left her there, the cemetery workers wouldn't notice her. Maybe they'd shovel the dirt back into the hole, and she would be buried with Ben, where she belonged.

one

It was the end of April, and Ben had been dead for six months when the phone rang late on a cool, rainy Thursday evening. Mariele glanced at the answering machine and shook her head in exasperation. She had forgotten to turn it on. She picked up the phone, ready to tell one of her more persistent clients that she didn't do business this time of day. She would tell them that they were free to either call back in the morning, or get themselves another decorator.

"Hello," she said into the receiver, not trying to hide her annoyance.

"Hello," an unfamiliar female voice answered, "this is Manhattan Hospital. I'm trying to reach a Mariele Hollander."

The room spun, and Mariele sat down hard on the side of her bed. This can't be happening, she told herself. Not again.

"Hello," the voice repeated, "are you there?"

"Yes," Mariele replied after a long, deep breath, "this is Mariele Hollander."

"We have an elderly woman here in the intensive care unit. Her name is Valda Novak, and she says that you're her niece. Her condition has worsened this evening, and she's been asking to see you."

"I don't understand."

"Please, Miss Hollander, we're very short staffed, and your aunt is a very sick woman. You're wasting both my time and hers."

"She's not my aunt. As a matter of fact, I've never heard of a Valda Novak before in my life. There must be some mistake."

The person who had initiated the call sighed audibly, and Mariele thought she heard her mumble something under her breath.

"You're listed on her admission form as the next of kin. There isn't any mistake. Mariele Hollander, that's you, isn't it?"

"Yes, that's me."

"Can I tell your aunt you're on your way?"

"Yes, I'm on my way."

The phone went dead, and Mariele pulled her nightgown over her head on the way to the closet.

Ten minutes later, she stood under the blue awning at the building entrance and waited while the doorman attempted to hail a cab for her. Finally, an East Indian driver pulled over to the curb, eyed her suspiciously, and asked where she wanted to go. He reluctantly agreed to take her to Manhattan Hospital before turning off his dome light and calling it a day.

On the way to the hospital, Mariele watched Manhattan's skyline move past the cab's windows. Rain poured from the sky, and they seemed to be moving underwater in slow motion. The skinny young man was probably not a good driver, but his vehicle might as well have had a life of its own. The cab's tires seemed only to skim the pavement as its passenger's thoughts were drawn back to that other night six months earlier.

She'd had her nightgown on that night, too. A sexy black one with thin spaghetti straps. She was sitting on the edge of the bed, setting her alarm clock for an early morning meeting with clients when the phone rang. She thought that it was Ben calling to tell her that he'd be later than expected. She smiled as she picked up the phone, anticipating the sound of his deep, resonant voice. But it hadn't been him. It had been someone from Manhattan Hospital calling to inform her that Ben had been in an accident. By the time she arrived at the hospital, her beloved husband had been pronounced dead.

The cab pulled up to the hospital's main entrance, and the driver reached over the seat to open the door. Mariele handed him a ten-dollar bill, slid across the seat, and sprinted the eight or ten feet to the automatic doors. A tired-looking volunteer directed her to the fourth floor, where she followed the blue arrows to the ICU.

Mariele approached the solitary nurse who sat at a computer behind the duty desk.

"I'm looking for Valda Novak," Mariele said. The nurse inclined her head toward the darkened room directly to the left of the desk.

The lighting in the room was very dim, and Mariele entered cautiously, letting her eyes become accustomed to the light. Only one of the two beds in the room was occupied, and Mariele walked up to it. The form lying under the covers was so slight that it could have been a ten-year-old child, but the face was wrinkled, and the eyes were ancient.

"You came," the old woman said, and Mariele nodded her head.

"You told them you're my aunt, but that's not true, is it?"

"No, of course not," the woman cackled. "You'd know if you had an old Aunt Valda about to die and leave you money, wouldn't you?"

"I don't understand why you wanted me to come here."

"Mariele, what a lovely, melodic name," the woman crooned, patting the bed for Mariele to sit down. When she had, the woman continued. "I am a psychic, Mariele. Not a calling I would have chosen for myself. Too much responsibility, too much knowledge of things that are none of my business. But that's neither here nor there. Like it or not, I am a psychic."

"Why are you telling me this?" Mariele asked impatiently. "It's late, and I've had a very long day."

"Oh, yes . . . I fear my long days are at an end. But that doesn't concern you, does it? What concerns you is that I have been in contact with a young man who is now on the other side. A young man who claims to know you."

Mariele knew that it was a foolish reaction, but,

all the same, her pulse raced and her heart beat with the rhythm of a jungle drum.

"What did the man look like?" she asked. "Could you see him?"

The old woman laughed, which launched a coughing fit that left her silent for long minutes afterward. "I have no proof of the color of his eyes," she said, "but he did tell me his name. Would you like to know the young man's name?"

"Yes," Mariele answered breathlessly, but the old woman didn't answer. The entire room was suddenly filled with a bright light that emptied the darkness from every corner. The nurse from the desk came flying into the room and stood at the old woman's bedside.

"Was that you coughing, Mrs. Novak? Well, I think you've really overdone it tonight. No more talking now, tomorrow's another day. I'm sorry, miss, but you can come back and see your aunt in the morning. Just look how exhausted she is."

"Let her finish what she was telling me, please. It's so important."

"No more tonight," the nurse answered adamantly, guiding Mariele toward the door.

But just before she left the room, Mariele heard Valda's weak voice saying her name. She turned and looked back, ready to promise she would return in the morning.

"His name was Ben," the woman whispered. "The young man's name was Ben."

two

The next morning, Mariele thought about the old woman immediately upon waking. She considered telephoning to check on her condition, but decided to make a quick visit to the hospital before her first appointment of the day.

It was harder to get a cab during the morning rush hour than it had been last night in the rain. But once again a doorman in a blue military-style uniform came to her rescue and used his magic whistle to attract one of the speeding yellow vehicles.

It had stopped raining, although the roadways were still slick with a mixture of rain and oil left by the thousands of trucks and automobiles that used the city streets every day. The air was fresher than it usually was inside the city limits, and Mariele breathed in it hungrily. The cab sloshed through the puddles left over from the previous night and skidded when it braked for jaywalking pedestrians. For at least the thousandth time, Mariele wished that she had someone with whom to share her love of the city.

When Manhattan Hospital came into view, she

thought about tapping on the glass partition to get
the driver's attention. She could tell him instead
to take her straight to the highrise where her clients were waiting to hear her remodeling plans for
their luxurious eight-room apartment. She had
loved Ben dearly, and she guessed she always
would. Still, maybe it was time to let go and move
on. Maybe she shouldn't be going to the hospital
to see some crazy old woman who promised to help
her remain in the limbo of grieving widowhood.

She didn't speak, the cab pulled over, and she
retraced her steps of the night before, steps that
would take her to the bedside of Valda Novak. This
morning, the entire fourth floor looked deserted;
she noticed it as soon as she stepped off the elevator. The doors to all of the rooms were closed,
and she was afraid to open one at random to see
if it was occupied. There were no nurses in the
halls, and no one sitting at the computer behind
the long L-shaped desk.

Mariele went to the room at the left of the desk
and eased the door open a few inches. The room
was empty, both beds stripped to the bare mat-
tresses. Valda Novak was gone. Mariele was wondering what to do next when someone cleared
their throat behind her. She turned, expecting to
see a nurse who would inform her that Mrs. Novak
had been moved to another room. Instead, she
came face to face with a strikingly handsome man.
He was probably in his mid-thirties, with silvery
blond hair and transparent blue eyes.

"Are you looking for someone?" he asked.

"Yes, a patient, Valda Novak."

"I'm afraid you're too late, Mrs. Novak passed away last night. Are you a friend?"

"Sort of."

"I don't think I've met you before. I'm Simon, Mrs. Novak's son."

"I'm so sorry for your loss. Actually, I didn't meet Mrs. Novak until last night." Mariele went on to tell him about the telephone call from the hospital and her conversation with Valda which had ended with the woman's identification of Ben.

"My mother was a great person," Simon said, at the end of Mariele's recitation. "She never passed up an opportunity to help someone who might be suffering. She obviously thought you fit into that category."

Mariele raised up her hand to cover her eyes. "If only I had insisted on staying here last night. Now, I never may know if Ben was really trying to contact me."

"I may be able to help you," Simon offered. He reached into the inside pocket of his coat and handed Mariele a white business card. In elegant black script, it read: Simon Blessing, Psychic.

She raised her eyes to study his face, and he saw her confusion.

"Blessing is my stage name," he explained. "You might say that I've become rather popular with the uppercrust. Simon Novak wasn't quite ritzy enough for them."

"Mr. Blessing . . . can you contact Ben for me?"

"Well, my gift isn't nearly as great as my mother's

was, but I have had some luck contacting souls on the other side."

Simon glanced down the hallway and cocked his head as if to listen. Mariele still hadn't heard a sound on the fourth floor except the sound of their muted voices.

"Let me buy you a cup of coffee, and I'll try to explain how this psychic stuff works," he said.

"Isn't there some place you should be? I mean, with your mother . . ."

"No, everything's taken care of. It was Mother's wish to be cremated, so there will be no long last good-byes. She was quite old; most of her friends are gone."

Simon looked away for a moment, and again, Mariele thought he acted as if he heard something.

"Will you say 'yes' to the coffee?" he asked again.

Mariele nodded, even as she realized that she would be late for her ten o'clock appointment.

There was a coffee shop about two blocks from the hospital, and that's where Simon took her. Seated at a small table in the rear section of the nearly empty restaurant, he explained his mother's psychic powers.

"If she were alive today, my mother could put herself into a trance and make contact with your husband. She could ask him the questions you need to have answered and relay his responses back to you."

"And you? Can you do that, too?"

"I'm afraid I'm not that gifted. Most of my abilities are appropriate for high-society parties. My seances are performances, planned after examining the guest lists and doing a little investigating into the guests' backgrounds ahead of time."

"Oh." She knew how her voice sounded, but giving up on Simon was giving up on Ben, and that wasn't easy.

"I admit I'm not quite what they think I am, but I'm not a complete waste either. Your dead husband found my mother someway. If he can find me, I will be prepared to take his message. If I know someone from the other side is trying to speak through me, I try and keep the channels open. That's about the best I can do, but if you can live with that—"

"Thank you, Simon." Impulsively, Mariele reached for his hand and lifted it to her lips. "I don't know why I want to do this. I don't even know what I want to come of it. I only know that I need to hear whatever it is Ben wants to tell me."

"I'll do the best I can," Simon promised solemnly.

Mariele didn't know what she expected from Simon, but she didn't expect complete silence, which was what she got. It was as if he'd dug a hole and crawled into it, then pulled the earth inside after him. He didn't call, and his telephone went unanswered. The days passed slowly and were made bearable only by her work, which was an emotional release as well as a creative outlet. A week crawled

by, then two. A third had begun before she finally
heard from Simon. Even then, it wasn't what she
had expected.

"Mariele?" He said her name the second she
picked up the phone, before she had time to say
hello. His voice sounded weak, as if he had been
sick, but she was sure it was him.

"Simon?"

"You have a great ear."

"I didn't think you'd call."

"You mean you'd given up on me. Sorry. I tried
to warn you that I couldn't control these things."

"Did Ben contact you? Is that why you're calling?"

"Your voice sounds warm and husky when you
say his name. Did you really love him that much?"

"Please.

"Yes, damn it, he did contact me." The anger
in his voice frightened Mariele to silence. "Sorry,"
he said, after a minute, "but I've been in bed all
day—hungry, totally exhausted—all due to a charming conversation with your Ben."

"Well," Simon said, interrupting his own tirade,
"can you come over here and fix me something to
eat, or are you going to ignore me and let me starve
to death?"

Either he was a very good actor or his voice was
actually getting weaker.

"Of course, I'll come. Give me your address."

"I gave you my business card at the hospital. I
hope you had the presence of mind to keep it."

Simon hung up, and Mariele spent a fearful five

minutes going through pockets until she located
his business card. She removed the suit she'd worn
to work that day and pulled on a pair of comfortable beige gaberdine trousers. The evening was
cool enough for a yellow fisherman sweater.

Having made it to the elevator within fifteen
minutes of Simon's call, her next problem was
whether or not to stop for groceries on the way to
Simon's apartment or see what he had on hand.
Assuming that he was a bachelor and further assuming that he really needed sustenance, she
walked down the block to a D'Agostino's. She
wheeled a cart around the gourmet supermarket
and filled it with basics: tea, bread, eggs, cheese,
fruit, and a bag of salad greens.

Outside, she flagged down the first taxi and directed the driver to the address on Simon's card.
She tapped her fingers nervously on the brown bag
as the cab sped downtown.

"Are you sure this is the address I gave you?"
she asked, when the cab pulled up in front of a
seedy looking brownstone.

"Two-nine-four-zero, et cetera, et cetera. This is
the place, lady. You stayin' or goin' back?" the
young Hispanic driver asked.

"Staying, I guess."

She carried the brown grocery bag with her
through the unlocked outer door and pushed the
buzzer beneath the name Simon Blessing. Once
she had pushed it several times without a respond-
ing buzz, she tried the inside door and found that
it, too, was unlocked.

Finding Simon's apartment wasn't as hard as she had thought it might be. His name was printed in black letters on a gold plaque nailed to the door of his second-floor apartment.

Mariele knocked lightly, then pushed the door. It didn't surprise her that it opened at her touch.

"Simon? Are you here? Simon?"

She walked through a living room that was tastefully furnished in shades of blue and gray, a sharp contrast to the outside of the building. Behind that, she found a tiny, well-equipped kitchen, where she left the bag of groceries on a butcher-block table. To the left was a short hallway, with doors leading off to a bathroom, to what appeared to be an office, and to the room where she found Simon.

"Help," he said, when he saw her standing in the doorway. He smiled, but the word was there, hanging in the air between them, speaking volumes about his situation. At first, Mariele was hesitant to touch him. He was a strange man, an attractive man, and she hadn't been close to a man since Ben's death.

Simon was wearing silk pajamas buttoned up to his neck, and his limbs were tangled in several blankets. Mariele overcame her reluctance, released him from his cocoon, and propped him up with pillows she'd found in the living room. She sponged off his face, while he watched her with his intense blue eyes.

"Are you hungry?" she asked, when he sat clean and tidy in his straightened bed.

"Famished."

"I didn't know what you had in the house—"

"I don't remember. Not much, probably."

"I stopped at the market, but I didn't know what you like."

"Anything." He seemed to be tiring again from their brief conversation.

She left him alone in the bedroom while she prepared an omelette with the eggs and cheese she had brought and a little leftover broccoli she found in the nearly empty refrigerator. She put that on a plate with toast and sliced fruit and placed the plate on a red lacquered tray. Meanwhile, she heated two cups of water for tea. Since she couldn't find any napkins, she added two folded paper towels, tea bags, and sweetener.

Simon was slumped over in the bed when she entered his bedroom with the tray. She had to set it down and lift him, waking him in the process.

"I'm sorry for waking you."

"I feel as if I must be in heaven, being awakened by an angel."

She blushed and moved the tray to Simon's nightstand, so that he could reach it.

"This is superb," he said, after he had swallowed the first bite of the omelette. Mariele noticed that his hands were shaky and some of the egg fell back onto the plate. Other than that, he wasn't as bad as she'd expected by the sound of his voice on the telephone.

He ate silently, greedily, and she let him finish before she asked him about Ben.

"It was sometime early this morning. I woke from a sound sleep with the sensation that someone was here in the room with me. I wasn't prepared, and he slammed into my mind with such force that I nearly blacked out. He just wailed at first, then he said your name over and over. I couldn't get him to stop, and I thought that would be the end of it. Then, gradually, he started to say something else."

"What? What else did he say? Are you going to tell me?"

Simon was watching her closely, gauging her reaction to what he had told her so far. She was almost out of patience with him when he spoke again.

"He said 'graythings.' "

"What does that mean?"

"I asked him that same question over and over, but he just kept repeating it until he was practically incoherent. The word obviously has a very bad connotation for him."

"Didn't he say anything else?"

"That was all he said until his voice started to fade in and out, then it faded completely."

"Graythings?"

Simon nodded and let his head rest against the pillows, as if merely repeating his one-sided conversation with Ben was exhausting.

"I know you're disappointed, Mariele, but he'll contact me again."

"How can you be sure?"

"Trust me, I'm sure."

"I'd better go home now, so that you can get some rest."

"No! You can't leave me." Simon clutched at her hand, and Mariele was reminded of his mother's birdlike claw. "You must stay with me tonight," he begged. "If he comes back now, before my strength has returned, the strain could kill me."

"But how will my being here help?"

"He won't come if you're here."

"How do you know?"

"They never do."

Simon closed his eyes, and within minutes, Mariele could see that he was sleeping. She pulled the blankets over his shoulders, carried the tray to the kitchen, and cleaned up after his meal. When she returned to the bedroom, she turned off the light and dragged an overstuffed chair to the side of Simon's bed.

Darkness engulfed the bedroom, and Mariele felt as if she were closed up in a black box. She couldn't distinguish the windows from the walls, or pick out Simon's sleeping form from the darkness on the empty side of his bed. Holding up her own hand in front of her face and trying to see it was an exercise in futility.

As she sat there in midnight's unyielding blackness, she thought of Ben. Simon had said that he was "wailing." She couldn't imagine Ben sobbing or crying, let alone wailing. She also couldn't imagine sharp, articulate Ben being practically incoherent.

There was one very important question here:

Had Ben really contacted Simon, or was Simon giving an Academy Award-winning performance for her benefit? Somehow, she would have to find out. Before this thing went any further, she would have to find a way to prove that it really was Ben who wanted to make contact, if, indeed, it was anyone at all.

And that word he kept repeating. Was it graythings? That was something else she'd have to find out—what they were, and what they had to do with Ben.

three

With the exception of Mariele's struggle with the veracity of Simon's encounter with a visitor from the other side, the night was uneventful.

She woke up when she heard Simon stirring, and she opened her eyes when he returned from the bathroom in his maroon bathrobe and stopped beside her chair.

"You could have shared the bed with me," he said, leaning down to kiss her cheek as if they were old friends instead of recent acquaintances. "I was in no shape to be anything other than a perfect gentleman."

"I was comfortable here," she lied. Simon smiled when she rose stiff-legged from the chair and hobbled toward the bathroom.

Over coffee, which he insisted on making for her, Mariele tried to keep her fears to herself and take what had happened the previous night as matter-of-factly as Simon was taking it this morning.

"What will happen now?" she asked naively. "Should I stay here with you today, or will you be all right alone?"

Simon waved her concerns away. "Go on about

your business, by all means. I apologize for acting like a baby last night. It must seem as if I disrupted your life for nothing, but all of my nights are not so peaceful."

"What will happen now?" Mariele asked again, when she stood at the open front door, ready to leave.

"We wait. That's all we can do. I'll keep in touch."

"Thank you, Simon."

She was an hour late for her initial appointment with clients who were thinking of remodeling an old brownstone similar to the one in which Simon lived, but it was in a different part of the city. Her heart wasn't in her work once she finally had arrived, and it didn't surprise her to learn several days later that they had decided to go with another decorator.

The message Simon had brought from Ben was insignificant, but still, it was good to know that some part of him lived. He had promised that they would live on after the death of their mortal bodies, and Mariele wanted to believe him. If Ben talked to Simon again, maybe he would offer definitive proof that his beliefs had been vindicated. She waited eagerly for the next contact, and it was difficult to settle down and concentrate on her work. Did it really matter whether the Johnsons polished their hardwood floors or had them covered with wall-to-wall carpeting? What mattered was Ben and what waited for her on the other side.

* * *

One afternoon, Mariele visited the warehouse she shared with several other independent decorators. A sleek gray sofa she'd ordered for the high-rise apartment job had just arrived from the manufacturer. It reminded her of the furniture in Simon's apartment and, consequently, of Simon. Ten days had passed since she'd spent the night in his overstuffed chair, and she hadn't heard a word from him. She ran her hand across the smooth gray silk and reasoned that he would have called her if he'd been contacted again. But what if . . . she let herself wonder what would happen if Simon couldn't contact her.

She left the warehouse immediately and walked briskly two blocks west to the parking space where she had left her car only minutes before. After the first contact with Ben, she had taken the Nissan out of the garage and started driving it to work every day. Hoping to be able to get around the city as quickly as possible.

New York City traffic was horrendous, however, and she began to have second thoughts about her decision.

It was only late afternoon when Mariele arrived at Simon's apartment, but the house looked deserted, the hallways dark and quiet. The doors were all unlocked, as they had been the first time she'd visited, and Mariele felt her way up the shadowy staircase to the second floor.

Simon was there, sick and debilitated. The odor

of his sickness assailed Mariele's nostrils the second she opened the door and gagged her as she hurried to open blinds and raise windows to air out the apartment.

The light, weak as it was, made Simon wince and turn away from it but not so quickly that Mariele didn't see his face. There were dark rings around his eyes, and gray splotches on his cheeks and forehead. Small flecks of bright red marked the top of his pale blue pajamas.

"My God, what happened to you?" Mariele tried to turn him over onto his back so that she could see his face, but he resisted. "Were you mugged?"

He nodded his head slightly.

"Do you know who did it?"

He nodded again.

"Do you want me to call the police?"

"They'd only laugh at you. Can you please stop asking so many questions and fix me some tea. There's some noodle soup in a container in the freezer."

She already knew that Simon was stubborn. It was probably wiser to feed him first, then try to get the name of his attacker out of him. Not that she cared so much who had done it. It was just so horrible that it had happened at all. The microwave sped up the process of preparing a hot meal. "Napkins, spoon, tea, sweetener." Her chant filled up the empty kitchen as she prepared the food.

Once Simon was sitting up in bed with the tray resting on his knees, Mariele thought it was time to start interrogating him again.

"Who did this to you, Simon? Your face is covered with bruises, and I can tell from the way you're eating that your mouth hurts. You can't let someone get away with this."

"I'm flattered by your concern, but you mustn't worry about me. I've survived worse than this, believe me."

"Maybe so, but—"

"Please, let it drop."

She shrugged and told herself that it was, after all, Simon's body and his problem. If he didn't want the police involved, maybe he had a good reason. Anyway, it wasn't her place to interfere and insist that he take action.

"Maybe I shouldn't be here," she said, standing and moving away from the chair where she'd been sitting beside the bed.

"Yes, you should." Simon placed his cup on the tray and pushed it away from himself. When Mariele started to reach for it, he stayed her hand.

"Ben came again last night," he said, and if he was looking for a reaction, he got one.

She took a few steps backward and let herself fall into the chair. Her breath caught in her throat, and she expelled it noisily. "What did he say?" she asked.

"In a way, it was easier than the first time. We almost had a conversation."

"Tell me, please."

"He asked for you several times, and I had to repeatedly inform him that you weren't here. Then, he said, 'Tell her, tell her,' and I agreed that I would pass on any message he wanted to give me.

"He started talking about 'graythings,' again and I must admit that the tone of his voice sent chills down my spine."

"I wish I could hear his voice," Mariele said passionately. "Isn't there some way I can hear his voice?"

"I'm afraid that's impossible."

"But he wants to talk to me, doesn't he?"

"I imagine he does."

"Why are you any different than me? If you could train me to be a conductor for psychic messages, wouldn't Ben pick up on that?"

Simon shook his head, and she lost her temper. "Well, why the hell not? What makes you so special?"

"You're asking the impossible of me, Mariele, and then getting angry with me for being honest with you. I don't want to have to refuse to accept Ben's messages, but if this is going to be your attitude, I'm afraid I'll have to do just that."

She slid out of the chair and sank to the floor at Simon's feet. "Forgive me, Simon. Don't turn Ben away. Please promise me that you won't do that." She sobbed hysterically, and when Simon put his arms around her and clasped her to his chest, she felt immeasurably comforted. She felt for a moment that he was a god, and she his piteous subject.

Mariele slept in Simon's bed that night. She fell asleep with his arm draped across her shoulders and slept soundly for several hours. When she woke up, Simon had turned away from her. He was lying flat on his back on the other side of the bed, his arms and legs flailing. He was cursing, and his forehead was covered with sweat.

"Keep them away from me," he ordered so forcefully that Mariele turned and looked into the dark corners of the room. Then, he said something that made her blood run cold.

"Ben, get them away from me. Offer them something else. I'm warning you, Ben, keep them away from me, or I'll—"

Simon obviously stopped to listen to the response to his demands, and Mariele found herself listening for the sound of Ben's voice. But it was Simon who spoke again. "I still have power. I have not been defeated yet."

Her hand trembled as Mariele reached across Simon's writhing body and pushed the switch on his bedside lamp. The bed swam in a pool of warm light, which pushed whatever had been tormenting Simon back into the dark recesses of his mind.

"Mariele? Thank God you're here. It could have gone on for hours if you hadn't been here to stop it."

Simon sat up in bed and fell against Mariele, nearly toppling her from the bed. He was visibly upset, and he was scaring her more than he could imagine.

"I heard you talking to Ben," she said.

"Don't be afraid," he murmured, clinging to her with clammy hands that left damp blotches on her skin. "It's me they want, not you."

"Who wants you?" she asked, as she tried to extricate herself from Simon's embrace. "Is it Ben?"

"Ben was here," Simon answered excitedly. "Yes, Ben was here. Did you see him?"

"No," Mariele whispered. She longed for her own bed but was afraid to leave Simon, even if he would let her.

Finally, she was able to quiet him. His rapid breathing slowed, and he fell into an exhausted sleep in her arms. She leaned against the headboard and held him, and it wasn't totally unpleasant, although a few moments before his closeness had repulsed her.

Before falling asleep, he'd told her about Ben.

"Ben was searching for you, Mariele," he'd said. "He was crying because he misses you. He needs to talk to you."

"Why can't he? Why can't he just come to me and tell me what's troubling him?"

"He's frightened," Simon answered slowly. "He's afraid that if he makes contact with you he'll lead the graythings to you. He will do anything to protect you, to prevent their getting into your mind."

"Simon, I'm trying very hard to be rational about this. Ben told me a long time ago that if he died first, he'd contact me to tell me if there is an afterlife. Now that he has, I don't know whether I should be happy about it or not."

Simon started to break in, but Mariele stopped him. "Wait—I don't even recognize the person you call Ben. I'm not sure if it really is him. Even if it is, his messages are not messages of hope. It sounds to me as if he's miserable, frightened of gray ghosts or something."

"He's trying to warn you because he loves you," Simon said, when she had finished. "You can ignore his attempts to contact you. You can tell me to go to hell. You have that option."

"You know I can't just walk away from him. He was my husband. But he's starting to frighten me. *You're* starting to frighten me."

"I think that's exactly what Ben wants."

After this conversation, silence had filled the room for several moments. Then, Simon slid his head onto Mariele's shoulder. When she looked down, he was asleep.

In spite of the ordeal he had been through, he smelled of shampoo and expensive cologne. Ben had been dead for almost a year, and this was the first man Mariele had touched in all those months. It took a great deal of restraint for her to ignore his close proximity.

Sometime in the night, she awoke again to find him watching her. Even in the dark, she could see the silvery glint of his strange eyes.

"Tell me about Ben," he said. "Maybe if I understand your relationship, it will help me deal with him."

"I don't know where to start." She rolled over onto her side and wiped the sleep from her eyes.

"How did you meet him?" Simon persisted.

"I was fresh out of college, with big ambitions and no job offers. I was pounding the pavement, looking for freelance decorating jobs. Ben was teaching English at Hamilton High, making barely enough money to survive in the city. But when he overheard me soliciting the owners of his apartment building, he hired me to do his apartment."

"You must have made some first impression."

Mariele smiled, remembering her first impression of Ben. "He didn't tell me how broke he was until he'd spent a half a month's salary treating me to dinner at a high-class restaurant. By then, it didn't matter whether I did his apartment or not. I was head over heels and madly in love with him."

"He must have been a very special young man."

"Oh, he was. Ben was intelligent, witty, charming. And he was caring. Children loved him, dogs followed him. I must be making him sound stupid but he wasn't. He was wonderful. I could never understand why he fell in love with me."

" 'Head over heels,' " Simon repeated. "No one has ever felt that way about me." The tone of his voice caught Mariele's attention.

"Oh, that couldn't be true. You're such a good person."

"Not exactly what attractive young ladies are looking for in a man."

Mariele laid her hand on his cheek and looked deep into his silver-flecked eyes. "You're a very handsome, desirable man, Simon."

He took her hand and held it briefly before releasing it.

"Thank you, Mariele."

After Simon turned his back to her, Mariele laid awake for a long time, wondering what was wrong with her, or if maybe she just had given him the wrong signals.

four

Hours later, Mariele awoke suddenly and thought she saw a movement out of the corner of her eye, but when she turned her head to follow it, it was gone. There was a subtle noise, a scurrying away from the light. Whatever it was, it blended into the gray border on the edge of the dark. It waited there, she knew, for her to sleep again.

She reached over Simon's sleeping body and flipped the switch on his bedside lamp. A muted circle of warmth spread out and barely reached her side of the bed. Simon stirred, then settled back into a sound sleep. Mariele felt gratified, knowing that he slept more peacefully with her in the room. He trusts me to drive away the scary things that wait at the edge of darkness, she thought, remembering the thing that had scurried away when she woke up from her short sleep.

She leaned over to kiss Simon's cheek, which should have been covered with stubble, but wasn't. It was as smooth as a baby's behind, and parchment white. She touched it with a fingertip and swore that she could see a tracery of tiny bluish veins beneath his cheeks. She thought that Simon looked gaunt, and she pictured him as a penitent monk wasting away for the love of God.

If she hadn't worried about waking him, Mariele would have run her fingers through his long, silvery blond hair. She tucked her hand under her pillow to stop its involuntary movement toward the sleeping man. She had thought him to be rather strange when she'd first met him, and she hadn't thought of him then in a sexual way. Now, he was beginning to grow on her, and lying beside him in the dark bedroom was making her think about him in that way. Ben had been dead almost a year, and she hadn't been with a man since the night before his death.

But nothing happened between them. She was shy about making an advance, and Simon seemed to be totally disinterested. She spent three nights in his apartment, going there directly after work and dressing for work each morning in his small, bare bathroom. Another day, and then, she held him in her arms at night and comforted him as he struggled with the demons that crept in after the sun set, playing havoc with the shadows in the room.

Everything in Simon's apartment was becoming familiar to Mariele, and some of it was becoming dear to her, to the point where she hated to return to her own larger, more decorative quarters. It was this realization that caused her to declare her independence of both Ben and Simon and return to the apartment she had shared with Ben, while Simon still slept in what she had started to think of as "our bed." As soon as she walked into her own bedroom,

Mariele admitted that her sojourn with Simon had left her anxious and exhausted to a depth that she hadn't experienced before. She was glad to be home.

Putting both Ben and Simon out of her mind—even temporarily—wasn't easy, but she was determined to do it. Spending nearly a year of her life mourning for Ben had left her feeling old, as if she were to be a widow forever, forever robbed of her ability to love, or to receive love. A widow forever, dead with Ben.

There was no doubt in her mind that Ben's memory was dangerous when carried to extremes. And getting mixed up with Simon would be even worse. The man was strange, at best. He looked as if he might be seriously ill, despite his attractiveness. Mariele felt a definite pull when she was in the same room with Simon, and she couldn't believe that he didn't feel it, too. So, if that were true, why was he keeping her at arm's-length?

Anyway, it was best to stay away from him, to keep her distance. She didn't answer the phone when it rang and screened her calls. She needn't have bothered. There were no calls from Simon, either day or night.

The date came and went when he had told her he would leave for Europe, without hearing from him again. It doesn't matter, she told herself, Simon is only a conduit. I'll have to let Ben know that he can contact me without going through Simon, that's all.

Mariele bought candles, knowing as she carried the bag from the shop that she was being foolish.

If Ben wanted to speak to her, would candles make a difference? Still, she lit them, close to midnight as done in all the novels she had read in her youth. No spirit called on her. Not Ben or any other.

One evening a week after Simon's supposed departure date, Mariele arrived home exhausted. She had spent the entire afternoon searching for a special French wallpaper for one of her more affluent clients, and for hours, she had looked forward to kicking off her shoes, sitting down with her feet up, and nursing a cup of strong tea.

A strident bleat from the telephone greeted her as she entered the bedroom, and she bombarded it with the mail she'd carried up from the lobby. She must have forgotten to turn the machine on. It rang on, more insistent than ever, and she grabbed up the receiver impatiently.

"Yes?"

"Mariele?"

"Yes."

"You don't sound like yourself. Are you angry?"

"I thought you were in Europe," she said accusingly, sure that Simon was playing some kind of game with her, and not wanting any part of it.

"I had to cancel at the last minute—sorry I didn't let you know. I'm leaving tomorrow though, and I have to see you before I go."

"Simon, I can't."

"I have to see you," he repeated, emphasizing every word.

"Really, Simon, I'm exhausted. I've had a very trying day and—"

"Come within the next hour, or I may be asleep."

He hung up and the eerie dead air of the telephone line filled Mariele's ear. She even didn't consider not going. If Simon had a message from Ben, and if he really was leaving for Europe tomorrow, what choice did she have? She changed into comfortable flats, picked up chicken salad and a loaf of wheat bread at the deli, and flagged down a cab.

It was forty-five minutes after his call when she reached Simon's apartment, and true to his word, he was lying in bed. He had left the door unlocked, and Mariele didn't announce her presence. She stopped in the kitchen, made two sandwiches and a pot of Earl Gray tea, and served Simon in bed.

"You're here," he said, when she entered the bedroom and crossed to the windows, balancing the tray on one hip while she adjusted the blinds.

"You knew I was here. You probably heard what I said to the driver when I got out of the cab."

"Just running up for a quick romp in the hay. Pick me up in ten minutes."

"Something like that," Mariele answered, surprised at Simon's reference to anything sexual.

"I'm glad you came." He said that after she had served him the tea and had sat down in the chair that he now referred to as hers. They ate and sipped their tea in a companionable silence, one not quite as comfortable as it could have been if Mariele was not aware that he had some news to impart in his own good time.

She was surprised when Simon shoved the tray aside and rose from the bed in his paisley silk pajamas. He paced back and forth in the limited amount of floor space between the bed and the window that looked out into the courtyard of his building. Mariele had closed the blinds when she entered the room, and Simon's thin silhouette played on them as he paced.

"At first, I wasn't going to tell you," he said finally, "but I couldn't leave town without knowing that you were protected. Not that I can offer you complete protection. I can't. But at least I can advise you."

"Are you going to tell me what you're talking about?" she asked. Then, she blurted out what she had been thinking for the past several days. "It seems as if you're always playing games with me, Simon. I think you enjoy your games so much that it clouds your judgment sometimes."

Simon stopped in front of her chair and stared down at her for what seemed like several minutes. "You're being sincere, aren't you? You actually believe that I'm using you to fulfill my dramatic fantasies."

"That's not what I said."

"Well, it's what you meant, isn't it?"

"No, it isn't. I just don't like game playing. I never did."

"Not even with Ben? Wait, don't answer that. It's none of my business."

"Are you going to tell me straight out?"

"I had a dream last night." Simon sat down on the floor in front of her, crossed his legs so that he could scoot closer, and put both hands on her knees. It was a strange kind of contact, too intimate for Mariele's taste. More intimate than lying in bed with his head on her shoulder.

"A dream about Ben," she guessed.

"More than that . . . a dream orchestrated by Ben, in which he spoke to me more fluently than he has before."

"What did he say?" Mariele leaned forward so that her face and Simon's were only inches apart.

"He said that he loves you very much. He said that although he is no longer able to touch you, he touches you always in the dreams of the dead. He asked me to touch you for him, to lay my hand on your body, to feel your pulse, your heat."

She shook her head, but his hand was already on her thigh, caressing, drawing the heat from her body. Simon closed his eyes and sighed, and for a split second Mariele saw something of Ben take hold of Simon's features.

She breathed her dead husband's name, and Simon opened his eyes, driving Ben away.

"He fears for your life," Simon said, his voice further displacing Ben and grabbing Mariele's attention.

"That's silly, my life isn't in danger."

"Ben thinks it is." Simon was doing it again, playing the game, making her beg for every tiny scrap of information. Mariele glanced at her watch and saw that it was after eleven.

"I have to go," she said, standing and brushing crumbs from her cranberry slacks. "I have an early meeting tomorrow."

"Very well," Simon answered petulantly. He stayed on the floor and let Mariele climb over him on her way out of the bedroom.

"Bon voyage," she yelled back from the door to his apartment. "Shall I lock the door for you?"

"It doesn't matter," he yelled back. "Do what you think is right."

She almost went back, to tell him that he was being silly, that he should act a little more like an adult. But if she went back, she would probably stay, and it was true that she had an early morning appointment with an important client. She left the apartment without calling for a cab, and she had to walk several blocks before she found one cruising for strays like her.

She climbed into the backseat of the cab gratefully and collapsed against the sticky plastic seat. She had become frightened during her search through the dark, silent streets, always aware of something hidden in the shadows of the gray buildings. Simon lived in a relatively quiet neighborhood, but she had never been there without seeing people on the streets, and hearing the grumbling voices of the street's unseen inhabitants. Tonight, it was as if something had driven even the prostitutes and the dealers into hiding. Something even they feared.

Whatever it was, Mariele felt as if it was stalking her and that it would pounce on her if she didn't find a way to escape it. The cab had pulled up just in time, and a voice that she thought she almost recognized had spoken.

"Cab, lady?"

"Yes. Yes, thank you." Damn you, Simon, she said under her breath when she had given her address to the driver and settled back for the drive home, what have you gotten me into?

There was a message on the answering machine from Simon. She must have switched it on out of habit before she left the apartment. When she heard his voice, Mariele pushed the save button, and left the message to deal with in the morning.

She slept soundly, probably because she was too exhausted to do otherwise. She was a little angry with Simon for dragging her out, only to refuse to tell her what he had learned from Ben. In the cold light of day, she admitted to herself that the real reason for her anger was that Simon had no news to pass on to her. For his own reasons (certainly not because he was attracted to her), he obviously enjoyed having her at his mercy. But as she'd told him last night, she was tired of the game now. She wanted out. She would push the bad memories aside and unearth the good ones of Ben that deserved her attention. She would struggle to get on with her life.

When she finally got around to pushing the play button on the machine, Simon's voice came through loud and clear. "Mariele," he began, "don't cut off this message because you're angry with me. You're right, I do tend to overdramatize. You have every right to be annoyed with me. Just hear me out, and then continue to be angry, if you feel you must.

"As I told you, Ben came to me in a dream last night. I believe he intends to contact you that way, but I beg you not to let him through. He is miserable and hysterical, and he still feels that it is his responsibility to protect you."

"Protect me from what?" Mariele asked, and uncannily Simon's voice answered her from the machine.

"From the gray world . . . from the graythings. He says that they are searching for a window into this world, and he fears that you will give them that window. He seems to feel that he somehow has set you up, made you vulnerable to their advances. I don't know exactly why.

"I wish I could tell you more, Mariele, but Ben began to ramble hysterically. I'll telephone you when I return from Europe. Meanwhile, what can I say? Beware of the graythings."

Mariele's finger was on the rewind button when Simon spoke again. "And, if you want my advice, beware of Ben's intrusion into your dreams."

five

Simon left for Europe in mid-September, and Mariele felt as if she was completely alone again. She had always been sort of a loner, and during her marriage to Ben, there may as well have been only the two of them alone in the world. Since his death, she had retreated from the few friends they'd made together, mostly other teachers who had worked with Ben. Recently, she had become rather attached to Simon Blessing, although she wouldn't have wanted him to know that, and she didn't actually want to admit it to herself.

She telephoned his apartment two days after the answering machine incident, and his machine picked up. "This is Simon Blessing," it said, sounding almost as familiar as Simon himself. "I'm out of town, but I'll be checking my messages every few days. If it's important, I'll get back to you."

Mariele was afraid to leave a message, even an apology. She had been sick of his games, and she had wanted him to go away. Now, he was gone, and she wanted him back.

In early October, she decided to try and contact Ben again. Not just the candles and whispering his name into dark corners of the room. This time she was determined to do it right. She cleared everything off the table in front of the couch and sat down on the floor before it. Then, she closed the blinds to darken the room and lit a single candle. "To guide you to me, Ben," she whispered. Then, she said it louder, as if he were standing right outside the door waiting for her permission to enter the apartment.

Waiting for him was a long, exhausting process. Her eyes grew heavy and finally closed, and her thoughts drifted away from Ben, to Simon, and back again to Ben. When it happened, she wasn't either frightened or surprised. There was a noise, as if the front door to the apartment was being opened and closed softly. A subtle stirring of the air, a drifting of the candle's flame.

"Ben," she asked, "is it you?"

The candle flame fluttered, and the air close to her moved but she saw nothing and heard no sound.

"Are you trying to reach me, Ben?" she asked. "Is there something you want to tell me? I wish we could talk, Ben. There are so many things we left unsaid, so many things I want to tell you."

The lights came on in the kitchen, and Mariele jumped up from the floor. "Who's there?" she asked, her voice trembling. "Is there somebody out there?"

She forced herself to walk across the room on legs that felt as if their bones had been zapped by a laser gun. The kitchen was empty, but there was an odor there, and she recognized it immediately. It was the way Ben smelled when he had been out running on a cold winter morning. She remembered those mornings so well; she didn't need the flood of emotion that came to her now to remember them. When he'd come into the bedroom and tried to kiss her, she had wrinkled her nose and pushed him away. "You smell like the great outdoors," she'd teased, and he had nuzzled her and kissed her until she hadn't cared about the odor anymore.

"Oh, Ben . . ." The kitchen door was unlocked, the door that led to the garbage chute, and she knew she hadn't left it that way. She opened the door and looked out, but the hallway was dark and empty. Ben wasn't there. She knew she wouldn't find him, no matter how hard she searched.

Mariele secured both doors and blew out the single candle that was still burning in the living room. She felt sure that Ben had been there, and just as sure that he was gone.

She went to bed early but couldn't fall asleep. She kept thinking about Ben, missing him. She admitted that she had felt a quick flash of fear in the kitchen, but it wasn't Ben whom she feared, it was the unknown. Whatever Ben was trying to warn her about, she knew that he was not a threat, dead or alive.

The next day was Saturday, and Mariele slept late. It was noon by the time she got ready to leave the apartment to do her weekly shopping. She set the answering machine. Maybe someone would call while she was out and invite her to a movie or a Broadway show. Not much chance, but there was always a possibility.

She lifted the lid and pushed the button to set the machine. It immediately popped back up. She repeated the process, but the button wouldn't stay down. "Now what the hell does that mean?" she asked herself aloud. She closed the lid again and gave the machine a closer look. No flashing lights, no beeping noises, nothing. She slapped it hard twice. The ancient television Ben had brought with him into their marriage had responded to that kind of treatment.

The thing made a whirring noise, as if a tape was being rewound somewhere in its bowels. She was afraid to touch it again. Things mechanical were out of her realm of expertise. There was a single beep finally, and then a voice. Or something that might pass for a voice. It said her name.

"Mari," the machine croaked. Then, when she was already reaching out to try and stop it, it finished her name, "ele." She froze, sure that no human had used a telephone to activate that cold, unfeeling piece of machinery. Her name was on that tape because someone who was not alive had put it there, to let her know that he had been there.

"Oh, Ben," she moaned, and the full power and gravity of the games she had been playing struck her.

That night she sat up, scrunched into a small space on the end of the couch. Earlier, she had gone to the kitchen for tea, and Ben's odor had filled the room again. Or maybe she had only imagined it? How could you tell if you were imagining something like that? Now, huddled on the expensive piece of furniture that had once been a major acquisition, a thing she felt she had to have to be complete, she felt that her apartment no longer belonged to her.

Ben had come home, and he had brought un-invited guests with him. Mariele could feel them in every corner of the apartment. Their penetrating eyes sought out her, and their cold breath brought goose bumps to her flesh. There were blankets in the bedroom, a pile of several just behind the left-hand closet door. She was afraid to cross the space that separated her from her bed, and rest, and warmth.

Near morning, it seemed as if the tension was suddenly sucked out of the room. The lights, which had been burning all night, softened from a hard glare to a rosy warmth. Mariele slid sideways and fell into a deep sleep, which left her stiff when she awoke several hours later. But she opened her eyes to her *own* apartment.

As she sat gazing at the morning sunlight streaming in through the windows, she couldn't believe that she had stayed on the couch all night, afraid to go to bed. Shaking her head at her own foolishness, she vowed that it would never happen again.

The next few days, Mariele threw herself into her work. She had a list of names and phone numbers of prospective clients given to her by people she had worked for in the past. She called several of them and set up appointments for the week ahead, filling her schedule to overflowing, trying to fill her life.

Nothing changed until the end of October, until the first anniversary of Ben's death.

On Halloween night, Mariele worked later than

usual, going over her books, lining up appointments, and doing anything else that she could find. "Busy work" her mother had called it, anything to keep from going home to her empty apartment where the memory of Ben would be overpowering.

It was almost nine-thirty when she stepped out of a cab in front of her building and took the elevator upstairs. The car she took was empty, and when she exited onto her floor, the doors closed quickly behind her. It was too late to retreat once she had noticed a strange looking man standing in the hallway, midway between the elevator and her apartment. He appeared to be waiting for someone, and he didn't look especially unfriendly, but Mariele never had seen him around before, and she decided to be cautious.

She made a point of fumbling for her keys, and she took time to look over the man carefully. He was young, probably in his mid-twenties, very tall, and well-built, or at least he appeared to be. He was wearing black pants and a black shirt, and he had a long black cape thrown over his wide shoulders. His hair was black, too, an atrocious dye job. She remembered that it was Halloween and let out a long, slow breath. Obviously, he was dressed for a costume party. Maybe he was even going to hit her up for some trick-or-treat candy.

When Mariele tried to pass him, the man smiled and stepped forward, blocking her path. "Mrs. Hollander?"

"Who are you looking for?" Mariele asked, stalling.

"I'm looking for Mariele Hollander," he said. "That's you, isn't it?" The smile had left his lips, and his eyes were cold and hard.

"Yes, that's right," Mariele admitted, "but I'm afraid I'm running late. My husband is waiting for me inside."

"Your husband is dead, Mrs. Hollander," the man said, and the smile was back on his lips again.

"Who are you, and what do you want?" She had taken a martial arts class when she was younger, and she remembered that her instructor had stressed the importance of being aggressive. "Don't be a victim," he had said, and she didn't intend to become one now. During the exchange of words with the man in black, Mariele had edged around him and had moved closer to her door. She had no other weapon but the keys in her hand. She wondered if she would be able to harm him with the keys, but she doubted it seriously.

"I'm not going to hurt you," the man said, thinking to reassure her. "I'm here to extend an invitation."

"A what?" Mariele asked incredulously.

"I'm here for an organization called the International Thanatological Society. Ben was one of our members. We're having a little service to honor his memory tonight, and we'd like you to attend."

Although the use of Ben's name had what she supposed was the desired effect, dropping her guard, she was still wary of the man and had no intention of going anywhere in his company.

"I'm very tired tonight, Mr.—"

"My name is Dwago."

"Is that your first name or your surname?" she asked, trying to build up the information she would have for the police when she reported the man.

"Whatever," he said, flashing the cold smile again.

"All right. Well, Dwago, I'm sorry to have to refuse your very kind invitation, but I'm extremely tired this evening. Perhaps, some other time."

"This is the anniversary of your husband's death, Mrs. Hollander. Are you seriously too tired to honor his memory tonight?"

"I'll honor my husband's memory when and how I see fit," Mariele shot back. "And how I do it isn't any of your business."

"I've tried to be patient with you," the man said, sounding not at all patient. "I told you I'm not going to hurt you. What else can I say?"

"I'm sorry." Mariele turned toward her door and had the key in the lock when she felt Dwago's hand on her shoulder.

"I'm afraid I can't let you refuse our invitation," he said, and she felt something hard poking into her back just below her shoulder blades.

"Just do what I tell you and you won't get hurt," Dwago said. His voice had lost its friendly, cajoling tone and had taken on the same coldness that emanated from his eyes. With one hand on her shoulder and the other pressing the object into her back, he led her back to the elevator.

six

In the lobby, Mariele tried to catch the eye of the doorman, who was usually quite friendly. But he was deep in conversation with another tenant and seemed barely to notice that Mariele was leaving the building in the company of a strange young man.

"Where are you taking me?" she asked, when the man unlocked the driver's-side door of a black mid-size sedan and ordered her to crawl through to the passenger's side.

"We're going to Jersey," he answered, with a narrow smile in her direction. "A ceremony is being held in your dead husband's honor, and we thought you'd like to attend."

They fell into silence then, maintaining it for the long ride through the Lincoln Tunnel and the drive northward into the affluent suburbs of New Jersey marked by exit signs on the Turnpike. About the time Mariele began to doubt Dwago's statement that they would be stopping in New Jersey, he exited the Turnpike. He guided the car expertly through a small town with pristine streets and manicured lawns, until the houses grew to modest mansions near the town limits.

Dwago pulled into the driveway of a huge English Tudor-style house, the kind Mariele and Ben had dreamed of owning one day. There were lights on two tall poles in the driveway, but no light came from inside the house.

"I'm not going there," Mariele protested. "There's no one home."

"Trust me, you're going in, one way or the other. There are at least twenty people in there waiting for us to make an appearance."

She walked up to the front door, with Dwago holding onto her elbow so tightly that she knew it would be bruised tomorrow. He knocked once, softly, and the door swung open. She saw no one when they stepped through the door, and Dwago closed it firmly behind them. He guided her down a hallway that ran from the front to the back of the house, with spacious rooms opening off to each side. Behind a staircase to the second floor, he opened a door that was flush to the wall and pushed her ahead of him into a large, dimly lit room.

"Dwago," several voices chorused, "you did it. You brought her." Then, from others came, "Welcome, Ben's wife, welcome."

Another man, older than Dwago but also dressed in black, took Mariele's coat, then led her to what she presumed was a place of honor at the head of a long table. Once she sat down, the others in the room took their seats at the table and waited for Dwago to remove his cape and join them.

"We are quite civilized," a pretty blond woman told her. "We meet in secret because our beliefs are not accepted by mainstream society, and we have no desire to make trouble for ourselves."

"Have you ever considered suicide?" a small, bespectacled man asked, leaning close to Mariele. "Pity," he mumbled, when she answered in the negative.

The meeting was called to order by Dwago, then turned over to a woman who was probably in her fifties. She, too, was outfitted in black, and when Mariele looked around the room again, she noticed that everyone in the room wore dark clothing. She felt distinctly out of place in her russet suit and buttercup yellow silk blouse.

The woman announced that this was the fall meeting of the International Thanatological Society, and that it was being held this year to honor Ben Hollander, one of their members.

"I didn't know," Mariele said aloud, then stopped when she realized that all eyes in the room had turned toward her.

"Many of our members are *secret* members," the gray-haired woman said directly to Mariele. "For reasons of their own, they don't feel that their motives for joining would be understood by their spouses or others close to them. Ben was obviously one of those who felt he had to hide his membership in our organization."

The woman turned and conferred briefly with a much older man sitting to her right, then turned back to Mariele.

"We certainly don't hold this against you, Mrs. Hollander."

"Thank you," Mariele answered, realizing as she did so that she had nothing to thank them for.

"People are drawn to us," the woman said to the room at large, "for many reasons. Sometimes someone they loved has committed suicide. Sometimes the writings of a suicide have seduced them, for example, the writings of Sylvia Plath. But, in most cases, as in Ben's case, they simply are drawn to the beauty of suicide as a moth is drawn to a flame."

Mariele shook her head, but everyone in the room ignored her. The other woman continued to speak, droning on about death being the ultimate challenge and suicide being the most courageous act of a person's life. When they had first entered the room, Mariele had felt a sense of relief. She had felt that even if Dwago were mad, surely there would be enough sane people in the room to outnumber the crazies. Now, she was beginning to wonder.

The woman rambled on, as Mariele followed her own thoughts. Suddenly, she tuned back in to what the woman was saying.

"As all of you know, we revere those of our members who have espoused suicide and carried their dreams to reality. Although they no longer can be present in this room with us, we owe them the greatest respect for having done what we desire to do above all else. It is for this reason that we honor our brother, Ben Hollander.

"Ben, wherever you are, we're proud of you. We congratulate you for having taken that leap of faith into the arms of death."

While the woman was speaking, someone had

been walking around the table, filling the wine-glasses that were set out at each place. Now, the woman raised her glass and waited for the others in the room to do the same.

"To Ben Hollander," she said in a loud, clear voice, "and to his wife, Mariele, who has done us the honor of being here with us tonight in Ben's place."

The woman raised her glass, and Mariele automatically raised hers, then took a sip of the tepid wine. Her head was reeling, but not from the wine. The things the woman had said—had Mariele misunderstood, or had it been implied that Ben had committed suicide?

She set her glass on the table, and it fell over, spilling red wine onto the white cloth that covered the table. She tried to pick up the glass, but it kept slipping out of her fingers. The others were sitting now, talking among themselves and watching her out of the corners of their eyes. They obviously thought that Ben had committed suicide, and she had to tell them that they were wrong.

On the night Ben died, a play had been put on by the students at his school on Long Island. He had driven there alone in his red Porsche because Mariele had a headache and didn't want to go with him. On the way home, he had fallen asleep at the wheel and plowed the little car into a wall at high speed. That was what the police had said, and that was what she believed.

A roast beef course was being served by a man who might have been a waiter, or possibly their host. The plates were already filled, restaurant style, and one was set in front of Mariele, piled high with slices of rare beef and assorted vegetables. If this was what she had been kidnapped for, they could have saved their energy. She had no intention of eating their food, when they had told such bold-faced lies about Ben.

"Excuse me," she said, loud enough to catch the attention of most of the diners. "Could I say something, please?"

Dwago stood and tapped on his wineglass with his table knife until he had the full attention of everyone in the room.

"Mrs. Hollander would like to say a few words," he said, and they all turned to Mariele.

"I don't want to eat your food," she said, surprising them, "and I don't even want to be here. You kidnapped me from my home and brought me here against my will. I didn't say anything because you said you were honoring my dead husband."

"Yes," someone said, "we are honoring him by eating this food and drinking this wine—"

"You would honor him more by telling the truth," Mariele yelled, cutting the other speaker off. "Ben always believed in the truth, and the things you're saying about him aren't true."

Dwago stood again and moved down the table toward her. "To which of our words do you object, Mrs. Hollander?" he asked, from the corner of the table. "Do you doubt Ben's involvement with our organization?"

"I don't know," she answered, "that could be true."

"What then?"

"You suggested that Ben committed suicide."

"Yes?"

"It isn't true. I would know if that was true. He had an accident. There was a police report." With every statement, Mariele's doubts grew. Dwago was staring at her with a strange expression on his handsome face, and it took her a few minutes to realize that it was a look of compassion. He felt sorry for her because she hadn't known. She hadn't known that her husband committed suicide, but they had known. They had been sure, beyond the shadow of a doubt.

"Is it true?" she asked quietly. Dwago nodded.

"I'm sorry, I didn't know," she mumbled. That was the last thing she remembered, except that Dwago suddenly was moving very fast toward her.

She woke up in the car just as it exited the Lincoln Tunnel on the New York side.

"Welcome back," Dwago said, not taking his eyes from the road.

"What happened to me?" Mariele asked. Her head was pounding, and it felt as if it might fall off if she touched it. "There was something in the wine, wasn't there?"

"There's always something in the wine," he answered, with the same sideways smile he'd given her before.

"I could report you to the police, you know," she threatened.

"Sure you could. Get the cops to open up your husband's file again, tell them he drove his Porsche into that wall on purpose. You'd do that, wouldn't you?"

She started to shake her head, but decided that the pain of movement was too great. "No, I wouldn't do that to Ben," she said.

They drove on for several minutes in silence, through the relatively quiet streets of the Upper West Side.

"It's nothing to be ashamed of," Dwago said, as they pulled up in front of her apartment building. A doorman she didn't recognize came out of nowhere to open the car door for her and walk her across the sidewalk to the building entrance.

"I'm not ashamed of Ben," she whispered, as she climbed out of the car. "I'm ashamed of myself because I wasn't there for him."

The doorman slammed the car door and the sedan sped away, leaving Mariele to wonder whether or not Dwago had heard her.

After a sleepless night, Mariele decided that she had only one place to turn for answers to her questions. She decided to try and track down Simon in Europe and find out when he intended to come back to the States. With his connections, he might be able to tell her something about the International Thanatological Society and its members. Maybe they were just a bunch of kooks after all, and maybe their accusations about Ben were groundless. The more she thought about it, the more confident she became that Simon would confirm this for her.

She decided to try his apartment. She was so surprised when he answered the phone that she hardly knew what to say.

"Simon, is that you? I didn't expect to find you there. I mean, I thought you were still in Europe."

"Un, no, as a matter of fact, I've been back for quite some time. Sorry, I didn't get around to calling you."

"It's all right. I mean, you weren't exactly under any obligation, were you? I know I treated you badly the last time we met, but I had lost my control. Do you forgive me?"

"I'm afraid I'm the one who should be apologizing, Mariele. But if you're calling about Ben, I have nothing new to report. He didn't follow me to Europe. Maybe his passport wasn't up-to-date. Sorry, I don't usually make bad jokes."

"Things have been happening here, Simon, things that require an explanation. Could we meet somewhere to talk? I really need to see you."

"I'm exceptionally busy, Mariele, maybe later in the month."

"A man waited for me outside my apartment last night, Simon. He was a representative of something called the International Thanatological Society. He kidnapped me and took me to a meeting someplace in New Jersey."

"He kidnapped you? Who was he? What did he look like? Wait, don't tell me anything else on the phone. Where would you like to meet?"

"There's a small coffee shop just around the corner from me. Would that be all right? Would it be inconvenient for you to come up here?" When he said that it wouldn't, she gave him the address and told him she'd meet him there in half an hour.

seven

Simon looked wonderful, and Mariele couldn't help but wish she had taken more time with her makeup. She hoped that he had missed her, but if he had, he didn't say so.

"When did you get back?" she asked after he had kissed her cheek and settled into the chair on the other side of the table.

"I uh . . ." he stammered, clearly embarrassed. "A couple of weeks ago, I think."

"You didn't call."

"No."

"Why not? Are you angry with me?"

"No," Simon answered, "of course not." He reached across the table for her hand and took it in his. Mariele, completely against her will, felt a small electrical charge at the casual contact.

"I've developed some financial problems since my mother passed away," Simon continued. "Unfortunately, it's taking a lot of my time and energy to straighten them out." He tactfully changed the subject. "Now, tell me what happened to you last night."

Mariele told him about Dwago, and Simon looked

on, open-mouthed. "It sounds ridiculous, doesn't it?" she asked. "Even his name sounds ridiculous, like something out of a bad B-movie. If he only had thrown in a few karate-chops, it would have been perfect."

Simon laughed and said, "Truth is stranger than fiction," before turning his attention to the waitress who had been hovering around their table. When she had taken their order and left them alone again, he urged Mariele to continue her story.

"The house was unbelievable—huge, English Tudor, exquisitely furnished, at least the part of it I saw as I was led in."

"But you have no idea what town you were in?"

Mariele shook her head. "None, I missed the sign on the Turnpike."

"But you weren't blindfolded or anything?"

"No, of course not. I hadn't even thought of it, but I guess he could have done something like that. That would have been horrible."

"Tell me the rest of it." Simon settled back in his chair and listened to Mariele's tale, making small clucking sounds occasionally. When she was finished, he nodded and started in on his salad plate.

"Well, what do you think?" Mariele asked. "Do you think you can check them out for me?"

Simon nodded again, his mouth full of tuna salad. "I'll see what I can find out. Now, eat your omelette before it gets cold. Could I have a taste of that? The broccoli looks delicious."

Mariele parted company with Simon at the taxi stand in front of a hotel two blocks from her building. He promised to get back to her within a day or so with information, if there was any to be had, about the International Thanatological Society. She truly didn't know what she would do with any information he got for her. For now, it was just something to do, like the busy work she would find for herself to do on rainy afternoons or snowy winter days when she was housebound.

She glanced up at the sky, which seemed to be pressing close to the earth, and started to walk faster. There was no rain in the forecast, but it was obvious that once again the weather people were going to be wrong. It looked as though there might be a cloudburst any second. The clouds were swollen with moisture, and the sky was getting darker by the moment.

Mariele watched the traffic for several long minutes, waiting for a break in which to cross the busy intersection up the street from the hotel. Safe on the far curb, she looked up at the sky again. Her heartbeat accelerated, and she felt the first symptoms of a panic attack. After Ben's death, she had experienced several of them, most having been triggered by thoughts of her bleak future without him. Now, she felt it again, the tightness in her chest, the pounding of her heart, the feeling of complete helplessness.

The clouds looked as if they were melting, that was the only way she could describe them. Parts of them were literally breaking off and floating down to the sidewalk, bouncing off the pavement close to where she stood, too frightened to run.

The cloud pieces that danced within reach were flimsy, tall, and willowy, and each had the barest hint of human features.

Mariele screamed, attracting no attention whatsoever from the hardened New Yorkers who hurried past her on all sides. She screamed, and she ran as fast as she could down the crowded street.

She raced into the lobby of her building, nearly colliding with a middle-aged woman carrying a tiny dog in her arms.

"Is there a problem, Mrs. Hollander?" the doorman asked, but Mariele brushed past him.

"I'm sick," she explained, as she fell into the elevator and punched madly at its buttons, hoping to locate her own number eight. Better to have him think she was ill than completely mad.

Inside her apartment, she stood in the middle of the floor and stared at the windows. The dark clouds were closer on the eighth floor, and she wanted to draw the blinds, to shut them out. But then she would be completely closed in, closed off from the light of day. The apartment would be dark, gray, like the floating pieces of cloud. What if they had followed her inside? She wouldn't be able to make them out in the corners of the gray apartment. What would she do then? How would she make it through the rest of the day, let alone the night?

Mariele sank to her knees and covered her eyes with her hands. She opened her mouth, and the telephone rang. There was a phone in her bedroom and one in the kitchen, and one on either side of the living room where she now knelt in the middle

of the beige carpeted floor. The simultaneous ringing of the two phones sent her scrambling to her
feet and racing to the kitchen to answer.

It was Simon, wanting to know if she had arrived
home before the rain started. She stood in the
doorway that connected the kitchen to the living
room and looked at the tall living room windows.
Water slammed against them in heavy sheets. Dark
gray rain, like the gray—

"Mariele?"

"I'm all right, Simon."

"The rain started so suddenly. I could imagine
you getting drenched to the skin with nothing but
that thin jacket to protect you from the elements.
Well, that's all I called for, to assure myself that
you were safe and warm."

"Simon, wait. You're going to call about that society for me, aren't you?"

"I'll do that right now, as soon as we hang up."

"Thank you. Good-bye, Simon."

The phone line went dead, but Mariele stood
there holding the receiver in her hand, watching
the rain that made her a prisoner in her apartment. She knew she could go out if she wanted
to. It wouldn't be the first time she'd done something crazy, like take a walk in the rain. But for
one thing, this was a real downpour, and for another thing, she was just as afraid of the rain as
she was of the graythings that lurked in the dark
corners of the apartment.

Finally, she hung up the phone and walked
around turning on lights, some that she seldom

used except on the darkest, dreariest days of winter. It helped a little, made her feel as if she had driven the gray demons back to their lair and given herself a temporary respite.

She made it through the evening and fell into an exhausted sleep after the late news. To her surprise, the complete darkness of the bedroom was not as frightening as the half-dark of the rainy afternoon had been. If the gray shadows were there, she was thankful that she couldn't see them. But it made her wonder how many other bad things lurked in the dark corners of the bedroom, watching her as she slept.

It was a long, sunless weekend, and Simon didn't call again until Monday evening.

"Did you find out anything?" Mariele asked after they had spent several minutes on pleasantries.

"Yes, as a matter of fact, I did. The International Thanatological Society was founded in England in 1970, and no one seems to know exactly when it started to accept converts from this country. The group you're interested in has been active for a couple of years, and meets in Fort Lee, New Jersey. They have no set dates for their meetings, and new members come in by invitation only. They're very secretive."

"That's all?" Mariele asked, after a few silent moments.

"As I said, they're very secretive. I had to call in a favor to get that much out of a former member."

"I thought all their former members were dead."

"Obviously, not all of them. The man I spoke to became disillusioned with the group after a few months. Still, he didn't have much of interest to say about them."

"Faithful to the end?"

"Something like that. They probably make everyone take oaths of silence to protect the organization."

"Is it against the law to belong to an organization whose members are obsessed with death? You know, they actually think that suicide is a goddess to be wooed and worshipped."

"That bad, huh?" Simon asked. "Well, I don't think it's unlawful, unless they're making human sacrifices or something. You know, helping their weaker members make the decision to commit suicide, or something of that nature."

"I don't know what to think. They were a very strange bunch, Simon. I wish you could have been there."

"Please!" Simon protested. "Don't wish something like that on me."

"I'm sorry."

"No, I'm the one who's sorry. Don't sound so down. You need something to cheer you up. How about a picnic? Can you take a day off this week?"

"Not really. Can't we have a picnic on Sunday?"

"No, Friday. Call in sick Friday."

Mariele had to laugh at his excitement about having a picnic. His enthusiasm was catching. "I can't call in sick, Simon. I work for myself, remember? But if I double up my schedule for the next few days, I should be able to take Friday off."

"Wonderful! We have a date for Friday, early. Say ten o'clock? No, that's too early. Make it eleven. Can you pick me up?"

"Sure," Mariele answered, wondering if he even had a car. But from what she knew of Simon, it would be just like him to take her on a picnic using her car. "Who's going to prepare the lunch?" she asked, wondering if it was in the plans for her to do that, too.

"I'll take care of everything, just be here at eleven. We'll have a great time."

"Where are we going?"

"That's a secret."

Before they hung up, Simon mentioned that he would make still another call about identifying Dwago and let her know the results on Friday. She wanted to say "No, call me the minute you find out, I can't wait until Friday," but she didn't want him to know it was that important to her. She would wait until Friday for news of Dwago. At least now, she had something to look forward to, a picnic.

On Thursday, she had a minor crisis at work, and she almost called Simon to cancel. Then, she thought it over and decided that she needed a picnic more than Mr. and Mrs. Cohen needed a Louis XV table for their sitting room. It had been a bad week, with her imagination running wild. She had seen wispy gray forms following behind her on the streets and waiting for her when she unlocked her apartment door each evening.

At least, the weather cooperated with her on Friday. The morning dawned cold and clear, a beautiful early November day. The sun was strong and took the edge off the chill that had settled into the city over the past few weeks.

Mariele found a pair of blue jeans that she hadn't worn since before Ben's accident. She stressed the word accident in her mind, refusing to acknowledge that Ben even knew the weirdos who had kidnapped her. She would never believe that he was their hero because he had committed suicide.

She put on a turtleneck under a knit sweater from Denmark, which was warm enough to wear in a snowstorm. Comfortable shoes and a Windbreaker to throw in the trunk of the car, just in case, completed her outfit. She was probably making a mistake. Simon would undoubtedly be decked out fit to kill. She seriously doubted that the man owned a pair of blue jeans or Dockers. Maybe he had been joking. Maybe he had no intention of taking her on a real picnic. He probably intended to take her to the Museum of Natural History or something.

She left home at twenty before eleven and enjoyed the drive to Simon's neighborhood. The traffic was light for a Friday, and the city looked its best in the bright winter sunlight. When she pulled up in front of Simon's building at exactly eleven o'clock, he was standing on the front stoop with a wicker picnic basket and a red cooler at his feet. He had an Indian print blanket draped over his arm. When he saw her, he picked them up and bounded down the steps. She thought again how good he looked, younger and more vital than he had before his trip. Something in Europe had been good for him. Maybe just getting away from New York had done the trick. "And maybe getting away from me didn't hurt either," Mariele mumbled to herself, as she pulled the lever to unlock the trunk for him.

Simon stowed the food in the trunk, climbed into the car, and leaned over to kiss Mariele on the cheek. "We're going to have a fine day," he promised. "Isn't this better than working?"

"Any day," Mariele confessed, pushing thoughts of the Cohens back into the little recess where she had hidden them and wondering if Simon had ever worked a day in his life.

She didn't want to ask if he had found out anything about Dwago, but Simon brought it up when they were in the Lincoln Tunnel headed for New Jersey and their mystery destination.

"The man who calls himself Dwago only joined the organization a little over two years ago," he told Mariele, "but he has a lot of influence. It was probably his idea to have the ceremony in Ben's honor and invite you as a guest."

"Is Dwago his real name?"

"No one seems to know. I guess you can join under any name you choose to use."

"Do you think I should file charges against him for what he did?"

"That's entirely up to you, of course, but if you want my advice, I'd have to suggest that you let it drop. I don't think they had any intention of harming you. In his own sick way, this Dwago character probably thought he was honoring you in some way. Bringing the police in only might complicate matters, maybe incite Dwago or one of his strange friends to invite you out there for another visit."

"And maybe they wouldn't be quite as hospitable to me the second time around?" Mariele asked, glancing at Simon's profile out of the corner of her eye.

"That thought did occur to me."

"You're probably right. In one way, I feel as if I were violated by that creep. But on the other hand, I feel that I'm lucky he brought me back in one piece. Maybe I should just forget it and let it go at that."

It wasn't what she had wanted to hear from Simon. In some deep place inside where old dreams die hard, she had hoped for chivalry, for protection. For "I'll find the man and tear him limb from limb." But that wasn't Simon's way. She knew him better than that.

It was rather disconcerting though, that he didn't seem to be very upset about her ordeal. Rather, he seemed to be intent on talking her into dropping the idea of taking any action against Dwago and keeping the police out of the matter.

When I get back to the city, Mariele decided, I'll have to spend some serious time trying to figure out Simon's agenda.

eight

Mariele drove south on the Garden State Parkway, which was beginning to look a little too familiar to her. After a few minutes, Simon directed her to pull into a rest area near Exit 155. A Greyhound bus was parked at the far end of the area. The sign on the front of the bus stated its destination, Atlantic City. Several dozen senior citizens milled around the bus, laughing and talking in loud voices.

"Park here," Simon ordered, and Mariele maneuvered her car into the parking space he'd indicated.

Mariele opened the trunk from inside the car, and Simon removed their picnic gear. He walked ahead of her carrying the wicker hamper and the red cooler, and she followed, the Indian print blanket tossed over one shoulder.

It was evident that Simon had been there before. He strode purposefully toward the restrooms, squat cedar block buildings nearly hidden from the parking area by heavy brush. At the last minute, he veered to the left and stepped into the line of trees that separated the north lanes of the parkway from the New Jersey landscape. When they stepped out of the trees again, Mariele gasped with surprise. They stood in a large meadow.

"This is beautiful, Simon, how in the world did you find it?"

"That's my secret," he said, smiling from ear to ear. "Are you hungry?"

"Famished."

"Good. You spread the blanket while I unpack the basket."

She laid the blanket out on the grass, then stood watching Simon work. The things he brought out of the basket were magical, pulled from out of nowhere by a master magician. But even more magical were Simon himself and the way his hands moved. Mariele was caught in his spell, enthralled by the golden breast of chicken and sparkling white wine.

There were white linen napkins in the basket and tiny tins filled with delicacies that she had never before tasted. Raspberries were the final touch, served with heavy cream that Simon spooned from a wide-mouthed thermos.

"This is the best meal I've ever eaten," Mariele said, lying back on the blanket to watch Simon finish his food.

"More wine?" he asked, and although she felt full to bursting, she held out her glass.

He started cleaning up, and when Mariele offered her help, he refused. "You've taken care of me when I needed you," he said. "Now I want to take care of you."

"Thank you, it's been a wonderful day."

"Mariele . . ."

The way he said her name caused something in her chest to move, and her breath caught in her throat.

"I have to talk to you about something important."

"No." She wanted him to stop, now, before he ruined the day. It had been too long since she'd had a day like this, or even a day to remember. Not since before Ben died.

"The man I first spoke to about the Thana-tological Society—"

"I said no, Simon. I don't want to hear it today."

"You have to hear it, Mariele. Anyway, it's not nearly as bad as what you must be expecting. It won't ruin your day, I promise."

She lay back and put her right arm over her eyes. The ground was cold, even through her clothes and the blanket, but it was better than sitting up and looking into Simon's eyes while he told her something she was sure she didn't want to hear.

"Ben was a member of the society, a very faithful member. He attended their meetings every month. No, don't look at me like that, and don't try to deny it. I don't know what he told you, but once a month he lied to you and told you he was going somewhere else, when in reality he was attending one of their meetings.

"He obviously talked extensively about suicide,

convincing them that he desired to 'embrace the goddess,' as they so quaintly put it.

"He advised them of his intentions before he had what you thought was an accident. If they're right, it was no accident, Mariele."

Mariele didn't move, and she didn't speak. There was nothing to say, as far as she was concerned. Ben did not commit suicide, no matter how many crazy people said he did. She lay on the blanket with her arm covering her eyes until she thought she heard Simon walking toward the restrooms. She moved her arm and caught a glimpse of him moving through the tall grass in that direction. That was the last thing she remembered.

When she woke up, Simon was gone, and the graythings surrounded her. They were in the air and on the ground, gliding from the sky on invisible slides and slithering through the grass like snakes. They were gray and lifeless, although they were moving as if they were driven by a propelling force. She screamed and tried to stand, but they were all around her, so close that she couldn't get to her feet without bumping into them.

As she sat there in the middle of the blanket, shivering and whimpering, her attackers became bolder. They inched toward her, threatening to touch her with their wispy arms, to bring their featureless faces closer to hers.

She called out Simon's name over and over, until he finally answered. "I'm coming, Mariele," he yelled, "hang on, I'm coming."

Seconds later, he was there, lifting her from the

blanket into his arms. "My God, what happened? You were sleeping so soundly that I thought I'd take a little walk while I waited for you to wake up. I've only been gone a few minutes. Was there someone here? Did something frighten you?"

She couldn't form answers quickly enough, but she tried to answer his questions with nods and shakes of her head.

"Didn't you see them?" she asked, when she caught her breath again.

"See who?"

"They were here, Simon, the graythings were here."

"Ben's graythings? The beings he told me about?"

"Yes, yes, they were here."

He took a step away from her and started looking around, giving attention to every tree and bush. Finally, he looked back to Mariele. "There's nothing here now," he said, almost apologetically.

"I want to go home," Mariele replied, and Simon took her arm. He led her back to the car, carefully, as though she were either very old or very fragile and tucked her in the passenger seat.

"Do you have a license?" she asked, when Simon climbed behind the wheel.

"Several," he joked. "One of which is from the state of New York. Not to worry."

He drove carefully on the parkway and across the bridge that took them back to the city. Under other circumstances, Mariele would have been exasperated and might have made the comment that he drove "like a little old lady," but today she appreciated his care in handling the car.

When they arrived at her building, Simon parked the car in the garage beneath the structure, although Mariele offered to drive him home. She was feeling better, less shaky and more in control.

"I'm coming up with you," Simon announced, as they entered the elevator. "If you don't mind, of course."

"I'd welcome your company," Mariele answered frankly. "I'm a little scared about what might be waiting for me up there."

"Poor Mariele." Simon bent to kiss her cheek just as she turned her head to look at him. His lips landed on the corner of her mouth, and she welcomed his sweet taste. She put her hands on his face and guided his lips to hers, their first real kiss, her first real kiss for over twelve long months. She leaned against him, but she was jolted back to reality by the bump of the elevator as it ground to a stop on the eighth floor. They moved apart, and Mariele led the way out of the elevator and down the hall. She unlocked the door to her apartment and waited for Simon to precede her into the small foyer that led to the living room.

He hung back and didn't meet her eyes when she looked at him.

"Is something wrong?"

"Maybe this isn't such a good idea."

"I'll make you a cup of tea, and we can talk. No kissing, I promise," she said, figuring that her sarcasm probably would be lost on him.

"I'm a very old-fashioned man, Mariele. My mother was from the old country, and she brought me up with a very strict set of values. There are many things that I don't take lightly. I guess you'd say that I'm a dinosaur of sorts."

He had finally walked into the living room, and he now stood beside a single chair, probably afraid that she'd follow him to the couch and sit on his lap, or something. She tried to be understanding, although it wasn't easy in her current state of excitement and confusion.

"Do you want me to apologize for kissing you, Simon? Or just for enjoying it?"

"Oh, my God, neither. It's surely I who should apologize to you. After all, we've only known each other a few months."

"This is 1995. Kissing on the first date isn't exactly unheard of." Mariele's mood was swinging back and forth between anger and amusement. He hadn't been kidding when he'd said he was an old-fashioned man.

"I'm sorry," he said, spreading his arms and raising his hands in a gesture of futility. "Now, I feel as if I've hurt you. Trust me, this has nothing to do with rejection. You're a beautiful woman. A man would have to be dead not to realize how attractive you are."

"Thank you. Now can we just forget this for tonight? Can I make you a cup of tea and talk to you about what happened today?"

"Tea would be absolutely delightful."

Simon followed her into the kitchen and watched

as she set up a tray for tea and toast with orange marmalade. Neither of them spoke for several minutes, and Mariele felt awkward working around the small kitchen with Simon's eyes on her every movement.

"Will you carry this into the living room?" she asked, indicating the tray. "I'll bring the teapot as soon as the water comes to a boil."

After pouring the boiling water over the tea leaves, she carried the pot into the other room. Simon was standing at the window looking out, with his back to her. When he turned, unaware that she was in the room, she saw his face. It had a look of sheer terror, and her hands shook as she set the teapot on the table. But Simon composed himself quickly and even forced a smile and a remark about the wonderful aroma of the tea.

"Is something wrong?" she asked, checking the window where he had obviously seen something frightening.

"Wrong? Of course not, this is lovely. Shall I pour the tea?" Simon bent over the table and busied himself with serving the tea and toast.

Mariele tried to look into his eyes, to see if the expression that had scared her was gone, but he kept his gaze fixed on the tea tray. She knew that he had seen something on the other side of the window, something terrible enough that he had had to turn his eyes away from it. And whatever it was, he obviously didn't want her to know that he had seen it.

Simon left an hour later, after two cups of strong

tea and several long silences, which did nothing to help them get to know each other better. At the door, he asked Mariele out to dinner the following Friday night, and she accepted his invitation. He kissed the edge of her mouth with his cold lips, and he ran his hands up and down the back of the silk blouse that she had changed into. Mariele wondered if he felt any excitement at all when he touched her.

While he had been in the apartment with her, she had pushed all thoughts of the graythings to the back of her mind. When she shut the door behind him, they surfaced again. The shadows in the apartment grew deeper, so that they extended into the walls and beyond them. Inanimate objects began to sway, as though they were being moved around by a giant ceiling fan. In her bedroom, the bedspread rippled, and the curtains pulled away from the windows. Pictures on the walls slid sideways, moving away from the living room windows. When she went to the kitchen to make sure that she had turned off the flame under the teapot, she lifted its lid and watched, captivated, as the water in the cold pot rose and fell, like seawater at high tide.

nine

The next morning when Mariele awoke, her first thought was a terrible one: What if Simon's information had been right? What if Ben had committed suicide? How could she find out without contacting the police and sharing her suspicions with them?

She telephoned Simon, but he had left a message on his machine stating that he was spending several days in Boston, "working," whatever that meant. Since it was only seven-thirty in the morning, she wondered if he had left for Boston last night and, if so, why hadn't he mentioned that he was going out of town.

Although it really wasn't a good time to let the business drift, she decided to take a day off from work. She felt that if she didn't get some answers about Ben, she would go mad. Stepping out of the shower ten minutes later, she could hear the phone ringing in the bedroom, and she rushed to answer it. Maybe Simon was calling her from Boston and just maybe she could talk him into coming back to New York sooner than he'd planned.

After her "hello," there was a short pause, the kind you hear just before the caller says "Sorry, wrong number," and hangs up on you. She had actually started to lower the receiver when she heard an unfamiliar voice ask, "Is this Mrs. Hollander?"

The temptation to say that she was not Mrs. Hollander was strong. The thought of spending an hour on the phone with one of her demanding clients made her feel ill.

"Yes," she murmured from habit, not from any sense of loyalty.

"This is Dwago. Remember?"

"Of course, I remember," she shot back. "How could I forget the man who kidnapped me?"

"Oh, come on," he drawled, obviously enjoying himself, "you wanted to go with me."

"Listen, you arrogant son of a bitch—"

"No, you listen. I felt sorry about the way we did things that night, and I wanted to talk to you about your husband. I got to know him pretty well the last year of his life. Maybe even better than you knew him. I thought maybe I could help you sort things out. But if you're into calling me dirty names, maybe that's a mistake."

"No, no, it isn't." Mariele spoke rapidly and with little control in her voice. "I'm sorry, Dwago, but put yourself in my shoes for a minute or so."

"You've got a point. Maybe we could sort of forgive each other?"

"I think that would be a good idea," Mariele said, thinking that "when it snows in hell" would have been a more honest answer.

"You want to meet me somewhere?" Dwago

asked, and her mind raced to come up with a safe
meeting place.

"Meet me in front of my building. I'll buy you
a cup of coffee."

The cup of coffee wasn't quite enough to fill
the bottomless pit that called itself Dwago. He ate
a breakfast that would have put a truck driver to
shame. Mariele wondered what he did for a living,
if anything, and how long it had been since anyone
had offered him food so early in the morning.

After he finished his meal, Dwago lit a cigarette,
without asking whether or not it would offend
Mariele. It did, but she kept her feelings to herself.

"You're being very patient with me," he said,
favoring her with a smile.

"I can wait a few more minutes."

"You loved him, didn't you?"

"Yes."

"He loved you, too. He never said so, but you
can tell, you know? He never looked at other
women, he never said he was unhappy or anything
like that."

"But you think he committed suicide, don't you?"

"I know he did, but that doesn't have a thing to
do with being happy or unhappy."

"You're not making sense." Mariele opened her
shoulder bag and extracted a twenty-dollar bill. If
she didn't like the way the conversation was going,
she wanted to be able to make her escape quickly.
Dwago looked at the bill in her hand, and she wondered if he was here to try and get money from
her, maybe blackmail her in some way.

"Just what is it you want from me?" she asked, waving the lone twenty like a flag in front of his face.

"I want to help you understand."

"All right then, help me, tell me something that will give me an insight into my husband's feelings before he died."

"He was obsessed with suicide, but not the self-destructive taking of life that most people think of. Ben wanted to free himself from the demands of life and exorcise his fear of death. He wanted to meet his end head-on."

As Dwago spoke, Mariele closed her eyes and heard Ben speak those words. That they were his was not in question. Dwago repeated the words, and his voice became Ben's voice, deep and resonant. And Ben's face rose up in her mind. She saw his dark curly hair, his intense dark eyes, as though he were standing before her again.

"Mariele, did you buy some more of that shampoo I like?" Undressed for his shower, body lean and firm, dark hair falling onto his forehead, he looked more like twenty than almost thirty. I love you, Ben.

"Mrs. Hollander?" Dwago was standing over her, shaking her by the shoulders. She saw him as if he were underwater, and she wondered where the water was coming from. That was before she realized that there were tears in her eyes.

"Dwago?"

"Yeah. Boy, you had me scared for a minute

there. You acted like you were in some kind of a trance or something."

"Dwago, if I ask you a question, will you promise to try and answer it truthfully?"

"Sure, shoot."

"Who sent you here today? Was it Simon?"

"Simon who? Do you really want the truth?"

"Yes, I really want the truth."

"It was Ben who sent me here. Before he died, when he was making his plans to go, he made me promise him that I'd make sure you were okay. He didn't want you to have any problems with his decision, you know?"

"Is that the truth?"

"I said it was, didn't I?"

"Then, I have to thank you for carrying out Ben's wishes. If you know more, maybe we can finish this another time, but I think I want to go home now."

Dwago walked her to the front of her building, tucked a tiny slip of paper into her hand, and said good-bye. In the elevator, she opened the folded piece of paper and read a phone number. Below it, two words were written: Call me.

"Is he flirting with me?" she asked aloud. No, of course not. He had told her the truth, that he was trying to help her adjust to the news that Ben had committed suicide.

She wondered why that simple fact was so hard for her to accept. Ben was an expert driver, and he had driven that same route hundreds of times. He shouldn't have lost control. He had no reason to be overtired that night, and as far as she knew, he had no weighty problems on his mind to distract him. So, why that night? She had to believe that he had been a member of the Thanatological Society. Why would they make that up? What good would that do them? So, he had been a member. To what purpose? It all made sense; she just didn't want to believe it.

On Thursday, Mariele canceled her dinner plans with Simon for Friday night and called Dwago instead.

"Feeling better?" he asked.

"Well enough to ask you out to dinner."

"That's the best offer I've had all week. Just tell me where and when, and I'll be there."

"My apartment, tomorrow night, eight sharp."

"I'll be there," he repeated. The menu consisted of filet mignon, baked potatoes, and broccoli with cheese sauce. She had watched Dwago put away enough breakfast food to feed a family of four. Feeding him would not be like feeding Simon, with his picky tastes and finicky ways.

She was right, and she had to admit that cooking for him was a pleasure. Ben had eaten only because food sustained life, not because he enjoyed eating. And Simon was always conscious of cholesterol and calories. But Dwago ate out of the sheer enjoyment of taste and texture. The filets were small, but thankfully, she had thought to buy two of them for him.

"I didn't think you'd be able to cook this good," he commented, wiping his face with a white linen napkin.

"Why not?" Mariele asked.

"Too pretty. Pretty women don't have to know how to cook."

"My mother wouldn't agree with you. She thinks everyone should know how to cook, even men."

"Not me. Not as long as Manhattan's full of restaurants."

"Do you live in the city?" she asked, and knew immediately that she had made a mistake.

"Yeah," he answered, then clammed up completely for several minutes.

Mariele made coffee and set out dessert while Dwago fiddled with her stereo system.

"Was this Ben's system?" he yelled from the living room.

"Yes, it was."

"He was always going to bring me up here and show it to me, but he never got around to it."

"Well, you're finally getting to see it," she said, over the thudding bass of one of Ben's old records.

When she returned to the living room, Dwago was standing near the stereo, rubbing his hands over the polished wood of the speakers. He sensed her presence and turned, smiling.

"This is some system. Ben always said it was."

"If you'd like to have it—"

"I couldn't afford it. Whatever you're asking, it would be more than I could afford."

"What I had in mind was—"

"Don't tempt me," he broke in again, "because I'm on unemployment right now, and that's barely enough to keep body and soul together."

Mariele set the tray down hard on the table, rattling the coffee cups.

"Damn it, Dwago, I'm trying to give you the stereo as a gift. Will you please just be quiet and take it?"

He stared at her, a myriad of emotions washing across his face, all of them easy to read—disbelief, pleasure, distrust, greed.

"Well?" she asked.

"Why? Why would you offer . . ." He paused and looked back at the stereo system, which covered half of one wall. "Why would you offer a few thousand-dollars worth of stereo equipment to me? You don't even know me."

"Ben did."

"But he left this to you, didn't he? He wanted you to have this after he died."

"I don't use it very often. To be truthful, I don't know very much about it. I just push the button to turn it on, then push it again when I want some quiet time. I'm sure you'll get a lot more use out of it."

"Boy! If you're serious—"

"I am. Use it in good health."

Two long strides brought him to the couch, where she expected a handshake, or even a friendly hug. Instead, she found herself being pulled into his arms and kissed with a passion that could not have been brought on solely by the gift of Ben's stereo system.

She struggled for a few seconds, then began to kiss him back. When his hands found their way under her clothes, she protested, but she was no match for him. Within minutes, her passion matched his.

They made love on the floor beside the couch, then moved into the bedroom, where Dwago ripped the covers from the bed and tossed them across the room. Then, he undressed Mariele, showing little regard for the fact that her clothing was relatively new and expensive. Naked, they fell into each other's arms and almost missed the bed in their haste to take up where they had left off in the living room.

In the morning when Mariele awoke, Dwago was gone. Her clothes were lying on the carpet in shreds, the coffee was cold, the dessert had congealed. And the stereo system was gone.

Her head pounded, and her hands trembled as she carried the tray back to the kitchen and emptied the stale coffee into the sink. Dwago had thrown the wine bottle into the garbage, and she removed it, to put it in the glass recyclable bin. Under the bottle, there were several small green capsules that she had never seen before. She picked them out of the baked potato skins and broccoli stalks and held them under the ceiling light to examine them more closely. It looked as if they had once contained a white powdery substance.

Mariele's head cleared a little, and she remembered some of her behavior from the night before. She blushed with embarrassment and looked back at the capsules she still held in her hand.

"That son of a bitch," she whispered. "That rotten son of a bitch drugged me!"

ten

Mariele's skin turned rosy pink, then deep red as the water from the showerhead pelted the soft parts of her body. She suffered it with her eyes closed, and she fought down the nausea that had come over her when she realized what had happened. It wasn't a dream, Dwago had raped her. From the way she felt, he had used her repeatedly, over and over, all night long. He had drugged her, then taken advantage of her, all the while bragging about his close friendship with Ben.

She turned her face upward and let the water hit her face and neck, to burn away the shame. Was I partly to blame? she wondered. Did I lead him on, or give him some reason to feel I wanted to be treated that way?

"No!" she yelled out. "No, I most certainly did not, and I refuse to take the blame for anything that sicko subjected me to."

Once she had used up all the hot water and half a bar of Irish Spring, she felt as if she might be able to face the world again. Still, she laid out dark clothing that would cover her from head to toe. She knew what a therapist would say. Well, let him say it! Gradually, she might forget what Dwago had done to her. Today, she could only remember.

Dressed in her bra and panties, she stood in front of the bathroom mirror and applied moisturizer to her face and neck. As she massaged the rich cream into her skin, she noticed a small red mark on her left shoulder. She shuddered and felt the nausea take hold again. If Dwago had left a hickey on her shoulder, she swore that she would find him and do something terrible to him in return.

She bent toward the mirror and looked closer. The mark was about an eighth of an inch long and was not sore or painful. It was in the shape of a teardrop or a droplet of blood. And it was definitely not something Dwago had made with his mouth.

She had to associate the mark with him because there just wasn't that much coincidence in the world for it to appear at the same time he had raped her and not be connected to that act. But if he had made the mark, how had he done it? She rubbed it with her index finger, and it felt slightly raised. It also tingled a little. She decided that it must be some sort of tattoo, done by Dwago while she was out cold. There was one other possibility: Maybe there had been someone else in the apartment. That also might explain how he had been able to haul off all the heavy stereo equipment.

The tattoo looked very familiar, and Mariele knew that she had seen it somewhere before, very recently, in fact. Once she realized where, she had to sit down on the toilet seat and catch her breath. A flashback came into her mind, and she saw Dwago undressing in her bedroom, removing his black turtleneck. She didn't consciously remember that scene, but it was in her mind, being played back to her with clarity. She watched in awe as the tall, dark man drew a willing woman into his arms. Her eyes were almost level with his left shoulder. She raised her chin and put her lips to the crimson drop of blood that was the logo of the International Thanatological Society.

Mariele dressed quickly and let herself out of the building. To go to work today was entirely out of the question, but she had to get away from the smell of Dwago, which now seemed to permeate every room of her apartment. Thank God it was the day her cleaning woman came. She left the woman a note to change the sheets and thoroughly clean the bedroom. She wondered only briefly what the young Hispanic woman might think about the stained, tangled sheets. Well, it really didn't matter what she thought, and a hefty bonus on her next check would make the nasty job worth her while.

Mariele hailed a cab and gave the driver Simon's address, before knowing that that was where she intended to go. Was Simon supposed to be out of town? She found it difficult to concentrate on everyday details. Her work was suffering; there were dozens of messages on her answering machine every night, some of them offensive, a few of her clients coming right out and saying that they would no longer require her services.

Until she could put her mind at ease about Ben and the circumstances of his passing, her clients could all go to hell as far as she was concerned.

The cab pulled up in front of Simon's building, and Mariele glanced up at the windows of his apartment. She thought she saw him there, holding back the drapes and peering down onto the street. But whoever was there dropped the drape back into place when he saw her looking up at him.

There was no answer when she rang Simon's bell, and no response when she knocked on his door. As usual, the door was unlocked, as if he had known she was coming. She stepped inside and called out to him.

"Simon? Are you home?"

"What is it now, Mariele?" He came out of the bedroom wearing rumpled pajamas and a ratty looking terry cloth robe tied too high across his stomach. A phrase popped into Mariele's mind: pregnant sparrow. Simon looked like a grumpy pregnant sparrow.

He stayed on the other side of the living room, as if he didn't want to get too close to her.

"Are you sick?" she asked, knowing that wasn't the problem.

"No, I'm not sick. Are you? Wait, don't answer that, there are so many possible answers."

He really was being nasty.

"I'll come back some other time. Call me when you're in a better mood."

She had her hand on the doorknob when she felt his fingers touch the sleeve of her black trench coat. His hands were small, with tapered fingers, and his touch was feather-soft. His gentleness endeared him to her, and despite his bad mood, she wanted to stay there in his warm, safe apartment.

"I'm sorry," he said, dragging the last word out, making his bid for forgiveness as dramatic as possible.

"It's all right. May I stay if I'm quiet and don't bother you?"

"Why do that?" he asked, tugging on her sleeve to pull her away from the half-opened door. "I want to be bothered, especially by you." They were so close that it was impossible for him not to see her eyes. It took seconds for him to register the pain.

"Oh, Mariele, you came here needing me, and I almost turned you away. Forgive me, please."

Her coat was peeled away and draped over the back of the sofa, and she was guided to a chair in the little dining alcove. Simon ran water into the flowered teakettle that sat on his apartment-size range and rummaged in the cupboard for "some special tea I've been saving for a day such as this one." When he found what he was looking for, he delicately laid some leaves in a tiny metal ball and lowered it into a porcelain pot, then added the boiling water from the teakettle. Minutes later, he and Mariele were sitting across from each other, holding hands and inhaling the heavenly aroma of his "special" tea.

Under these circumstances, it wasn't difficult for Mariele to tell him what Dwago had done to her.

"Bless you, Simon," she said, after he had summoned up all his masculinity and threatened to emasculate her attacker. "Even as I speak, I'm making the decision to change the locks on my door and write this off as a bad experience."

"Did he hurt you?" Simon asked, turning her arm over to examine her delicate skin for bruises.

"Only my pride," she answered. "Oh, I'm a little sore, but that will pass."

"No bruises, no other marks?"

"Funny that you should ask, because there is a mark." She slipped her arm out of her black sweater so that she could display the red droplet on her shoulder. Simon didn't take it well.

"I'll kill that madman," he screamed, kicking his chair away from the table and beginning to pace the room as if he were an animal trying to break out of his cage.

"Sit down, Simon," Mariele commanded, and to her surprise, he sat, taking up her hand again.

"I don't know what all this means, Mariele," he explained when he had calmed down sufficiently to talk. "And the timing . . . I was going to call you this afternoon to tell you that I'd heard from Ben again. Then, you walked into the room before I had a chance to compose my thoughts, and you tell me this completely wild story about Dwago. Now, you show me a tattoo that he obviously gave you while you were drugged. Don't expect me to sit down and take this calmly, please."

It was nearly an hour later when Simon got dressed and accompanied Mariele to a small park just minutes from his apartment. It was cold and the forecast called for rain. As they sat on a green bench and prepared to speak of the dead, Mariele couldn't help but keep looking up at the clouds that brooded above them. They were there. She was sure. When she glanced out of the corner of her eye, she could see their slithering shapes. The huge cloud directly above her head remained still, but the graythings within it jerked and wiggled and threatened to come floating down to claim her for their own.

"Mariele!"

"Sorry, Simon. Go on, please."

"I was telling you that I had another dream last night. Ben stood in front of a low stone building and spoke to me. He kept fading in and out, as if he had a bad signal. He called out your name and said that you were in danger. He said he had tried to contact you, but other forces were vying with him to get into your mind. 'The graythings,' he kept saying, and his voice sounded so plaintive, so lost. 'The graythings are breaking through into the world of the living. They want my Mariele.' I tried to reassure him, but he was wretched. There was no consoling him."

"My God, who would think that we would have to console the dead? Oh, I'm sorry, I didn't mean it that way. I loved Ben very much. I still love him. But this worry is driving me crazy. It's tearing me apart, Simon."

He took his arm from across the back of the bench and wrapped it around Mariele's shoulders. She laid her head on his shoulder and closed her eyes. Seconds later, Simon flew to his feet, flinging her away from him. She screamed, without knowing why she was screaming.

"It dropped just behind the bench," Simon explained nervously. "I swear, it just dropped out of the sky and landed inches from my hand. I don't know what the hell it was. Some kind of animal, obviously, something gray and slimy looking. When I jumped, it ran away, hid itself in those bushes over there. Do you think we should go looking for it?"

Mariele was too scared to speak, but she shook her head back and forth as hard as she could, and Simon understood.

"I didn't mean to scare you," he said more calmly. "I know you're already shaken up over what happened last night. I'm not doing anything right today, am I?"

"You're here, that's all that matters. Can we leave now? Could you fix me another cup of tea before I have to start home?"

Later, Simon flagged down a cab on the corner near his building and bundled Mariele inside. She asked the driver to let her off at a Chinese takeout about two blocks from her apartment. When the small white shopping bag was handed to her across the counter, she started walking toward home. In the restaurant, she hadn't noticed how dark the sky had become, or how close to the earth the clouds were hanging. She never before had suffered from claustrophobia, but now, she felt as if she couldn't breathe. A block from her building, she dropped the bag of Chinese food to the sidewalk and used both hands to claw at the collar of her sweater. By the time she staggered into the lobby, her neck was bleeding profusely.

"Are you all right, Mrs. Hollander? Should I call a doctor?" This was the recently hired young doorman, the one who flirted with her.

"What's wrong, Joe?" She couldn't see George's face, but she recognized his kindly voice. He had been on duty the night she and Ben returned from their honeymoon.

"I'm not sure," Joe answered, "but I think Mrs. Hollander got mugged."

"Move aside. Mrs. Hollander, it's me, George. Can you hear me?"

"She acts like she can hear us talking, but she can't answer or something."

"Call Dr. Rosenkrantz in Five-B. Then, call the police. Hurry up!"

That was all Mariele remembered until she woke up some time later. She was lying in her own bed, and a middle-aged man with a graying goatee was sitting on the bed beside her.

"Ah, Mrs. Hollander, you've decided to honor us with your presence."

"Who are you? And what happened to me?"

"The answer to your first question is that I am Bruce Rosenkrantz, your neighbor from Five-B, who just happens to be a licensed medical doctor.

As to your second question, we have been waiting patiently for you to tell us the answer."

"We?"

"Myself and the young police officer who has been patiently waiting in your lovely living room."

"The police?"

"George was frightened. It appeared as if you had lost quite a lot of blood. Actually, it looked much worse than it was. Still, there are questions to be answered. Shall I inform the young officer that you have awakened?"

"Yes, please." While her neighbor went to fetch the policeman, Mariele tried to remember what exactly had happened to her. She wasn't having much luck when Rosenkrantz returned with an NYPD officer in tow.

"Feeling better, Mrs. Hollander?" the cop asked.

Without waiting for Mariele's answer, he continued, "Think you can answer a few questions?" She nodded, and the questions started coming.

"Tell me exactly what happened this afternoon? Did someone attack you? Please, try to remember. Were you fighting off an attacker? Is that how you got the scratches on your neck? Were you clawing at their hands to try and make them let go of your neck?"

Mariele didn't know the answer to any of the questions, and she said so.

"We'll be in touch," the cop said a half an hour later. "Meanwhile, if you remember anything, call us."

After he had let himself out of the apartment,

Mariele realized that Dr. Rosenkrantz was still there. For a large man, he had done a remarkable job of blending into the background and becoming invisible.

He picked up his medical bag and patted Mariele's cheek on his way to the door. "If you need anything, pretty lady, you call Rosenkrantz, in Five-B. Anything at all."

Then, the doctor was gone, and she was alone in the darkening apartment. Alone with the wide expanse of wall-to-wall windows that stretched from the floor to the ceiling and exposed her to the clouds and to the things that fell out of the clouds and slid down her windowpanes.

eleven

Mariele ran out into the hallway in search of Rosenkrantz, but she was too late. The elevator doors made a whooshing sound as they closed, and the motor labored to carry him down to the fifth floor. She was definitely alone. There was no one to call, no special friend who might come to her rescue. Ben had been her best friend, her only friend, and Ben was gone.

It was simple to drag an easy chair across the carpet and position it in front of the living room windows. Waiting for the graythings was easier on her nerves than running from them. She laid her head on the back of the chair and let her eyes rest on the ever present clouds until they blended in with the blackness of the moonless, starless night.

Thoughts of Ben came to her as easily as they had when he was alive. He could do no wrong then. Whatever he did, she forgave him. If he acted foolishly, she called his behavior childlike. If he was irresponsible, she was responsible in his stead. She made Ben into a perfect person in her mind, and she projected this image to others. And she kept him in her mind always, as if that would be enough to prevent his image from slipping.

But this was different. What was happening now was definitely not the same. How could she continue to protect him? How could she save a dead man from his enemies?

Mariele sat in the chair all night, sleeping for short periods of time, then waking in fits and starts. The graythings were there, but she couldn't see them. She sensed them, and that was worse.

By the middle of the night, she had come to a decision, but she patiently waited for the sun to come up before dialing Simon's number.

His voice sounded crisp and fresh, and Mariele envied him. Had she ever sounded so normal? If so, she couldn't remember it.

"Simon, it's me."

"Mariele?"

"Yes, did I wake you?"

"No. Are you all right?"

"Simon, I need to talk to Ben."

"Mariele, please, I'm just not up to it."

"Once before you mentioned a séance, you said that would be easier on you."

"It would, but—"

"Please don't blow me off, Simon. I really need this."

"Call me back tomorrow morning. I'll see what I can set up." She tried to ignore the fact that he sighed as he hung up the phone.

Mariele wouldn't have thought that Simon knew so many people who would rally around him at a moment's notice, but by the time she called him the following morning, he had been able to gather six people to participate in the séance. They were to meet at ten o'clock on Friday evening, at Mariele's apartment. Simon said her dining-room table would do, but he advised her to rent some folding chairs, so that they all could fit comfortably at the table.

At the same time, she rented a thirty-cup percolator, hoping that it was appropriate to serve coffee and other refreshments at a bona fide séance.

It seemed like a long way to Friday, and Mariele veered back and forth between wanting it to come quickly and not wanting it to come at all. Ever. She expected Simon's friends to be a bunch of weirdos, dressed for the parts they were going to play. She was pleasantly surprised when she opened the door and introduced herself to six well-dressed, articulate people, most of whom displayed a sense of humor about what they were about to do.

"I want you to know that I usually only do this on Halloween," a pretty brunette said, "but I owe one to Simon. He got in touch with my mother once when I was in pretty desperate shape. He probably saved my life."

One young couple sat with their chairs touching, taking turns sipping tea from a single cup. They were silent and unsmiling, and their sad eyes kept watching Simon for signs. In the kitchen, he whispered to Mariele that they had lost their little girl and were trying desperately to contact her spirit.

After coffee or tea and a few minutes spent set
tling in, Simon called the small group to attention.

"We have a specific goal tonight," he said, looking from one face to another. "We will attempt to
contact Mariele's deceased husband, whose name
is Ben. I have already been in contact with him
several times, but each time he has been the seeker.
Tonight, I will seek to contact Ben. If I am suc-
cessful, I will pass the contact to Mariele, so that
she may speak with him personally.

"We have an article of Ben's clothing which we
will pass around the table now. This is a jacket that
has not been dry-cleaned since his death, and it
still contains his scent. As you all know, we have a
good chance of getting through to Ben if we concentrate our energy.

"Mariele and I both appreciate your coming
here tonight to offer your assistance. Later, if Ben
either does not come, or if he leaves us too soon,
we will leave ourselves open to anyone else who
may wish to seek us out."

Mariele watched as Ben's black leather jacket was
handed from one guest to the next. She flinched
when one man scratched at the jacket as if it were
a scratch and sniff air freshener, then rubbed his
nose back and forth on the leather. The pretty girl
with the dark hair turned the sleeves inside out
and buried her face in the lining. They're only
trying to help, Mariele told herself, but Simon
hadn't prepared her for their bizarre behavior.

Once the jacket had made the rounds, Simon
handed it back to her and took her hand. She no-

ticed that everyone at the table now held hands with the person on either side of them. She expected to hear a lot of mumbo jumbo. Her experience with séances was limited to what she had read in books or seen in movies. But to her surprise, the people at the table fell silent. The only sound she could hear was the sound of Simon's breathing, which became more and more labored. When he finally spoke, Mariele started, and he gripped her hand more tightly.

"We are looking for Ben Hollander," Simon shouted. "We wish to communicate with the spirit of Ben Hollander. Ben Hollander, come forward." Simon's voice was loud and clear, as if he was trying to be heard over a lot of background noise.

He repeated the same words over and over, until Mariele was sure that Ben couldn't hear them, or just didn't want to establish contact. Then, suddenly, Simon's hand jerked out of hers, and he fell forward. His head struck the table with a loud crack, but no one else at the table moved or spoke. Mariele sat still and kept her silence, although her first instinct was to check on Simon's condition.

She had heard the term "pregnant silence," but she hadn't experienced one before. Now, she understood what the expression meant. The room was filled with a silence so intense that there seemed to be one layer of silence on top of another, one silence ready to burst and shatter still another silence that was an integral part of the room. Had Mariele not known better, she would

have sworn that the room had never been blessed
with sound, or its inhabitants with hearing.

It was into this vast well of silence that Mariele's
dead husband dropped her name.

"Ben?" she asked. "Ben, is it really you? Can
you hear me, sweetheart?" She was aware of the
other people sitting around the table, most of
them still holding hands, some with their heads
bowed, some staring straight ahead. But she didn't
care if they heard her talking to Ben. After all,
they were here for the same purpose, weren't they?

"Mari . . . it's bad." Mariele couldn't tell whether
or not Simon's lips were moving, but Ben's voice
was coming from the area of Simon's face. She spoke
back to Simon, as if he were Ben.

"Oh, darling, I'm sorry. Is there any way I can
help you?"

"Too late for me . . . help . . . yourself."

"I'm fine, Ben, don't worry about me."

"Worry about . . . graythings. Graythings everywhere . . . pressing down . . . earth." His voice
was fading in and out, something that sounded
like static interfering with Mariele's reception of
his message.

"So close, Mari . . . so many. If you knew . . .
couldn't live with it. Help. . . ."

A blast of static ended Ben's words and brought
Simon's head back off the table. There was a lump
on his forehead, which was already turning black
and blue.

"My God, Simon, you've hurt yourself," one of
his followers blurted out, and the group trance was

broken. It didn't take long for Simon to find out what had happened, since everyone at the table had heard Ben's words and seemed anxious to relay them to their leader.

This turned out to be a night full of surprises for Mariele, the next one being that Simon was angry with her.

"I don't understand why you're so upset with me," she said, after the others had departed.

"Didn't it occur to you that it could have been a trick?" he asked.

"A trick?"

"Yes, a trick," he spat back at her. "It could have been someone else masquerading as Ben."

"It was Ben's voice."

"That doesn't mean anything. This is very dangerous business, Mariele, you shouldn't make light of it."

"You didn't tell me it was going to be dangerous. Why didn't you tell me if that was the case?"

"I thought I would be here to protect you, but obviously someone didn't want me around."

"Ben?"

"Or someone else."

"You're making this all so complicated, Simon. I talked to Ben, why can't we just forget the rest of it?"

"Is that what you want to do?"

She nodded, putting her hands together, and set her chin upon her fingertips. "Please?"

"Don't pray to me, Mariele, it will go to my

head." It took her a minute to realize this was his idea of a joke.

"Sorry," she murmured, lowering her hands and forcing herself to smile at him.

"It probably was Ben," Simon admitted as he helped Mariele clean up the kitchen. "Why in the world did you lay in so much food, did you think they'd stay and eat all night?"

"I didn't know. Take some of the chips and things home with you."

"I don't eat junk food, haven't you noticed?"

"This stuff is free."

"It's been a good year. I haven't sunk quite to the poverty level yet."

"Suit yourself." She stuffed bags of Doritos and potato chips into a brown bag for delivery to the doormen after Simon left.

"You're sure that's all he said?" Simon asked.

"Ben? Yes, I'm sure. He said the graythings were pressing close to the earth, and that if I knew how many of them were here, I wouldn't be able to stand it. Or something like that."

"I don't know how you feel, but he's doing a damn good job of frightening me," Simon said, with a shudder that traveled the length of his body.

"Simon . . ."

He stopped wiping the counter and looked at her, picking up on her change of mood from the way she had spoken his name.

"I'm so scared that I can barely function. I haven't been going to work, and I've been sleeping in a chair in the living room. I'm afraid they're going to sneak up on me while I'm asleep and . . . Well, actually, that's the worst thing, that I don't have any idea what they want to do to me."

"I think Ben's expression was 'infiltrate her mind.' "

"That is scary, isn't it? Why is it that I don't fear that as much as physical harm?"

"We all value our precious bodies, don't we? But imagine losing your mind, or your soul?"

"Is my soul at risk here?" She tried to keep it light, but it didn't work. "It is, isn't it?"

"Yes, it probably is," Simon admitted. He laid down his dishrag and opened his arms to her.

She begged him to stay the night, and he agreed gracefully. Ben's pajamas were too big for him, but they worked with the help of two big safety pins. He let her choose her side of the bed, then climbed in on the other side.

"Hold me," Mariele whispered, and she sensed no reluctance when he turned toward her. When she went further and said "kiss me," he did, but that was as far as he'd go.

"I love you in my own way, Mariele," he said, long minutes later, "but I'm not ready to make love to you yet."

"Will you ever be ready, Simon?"

"I don't want to lie to you."

She buried her head in his shoulder and let him rock her to sleep. It was the first good night's sleep she'd had for a long time.

twelve

Mariele woke up just as the sun was sliding over the top of Manhattan's skyscrapers. Pale morning light crept around the edges of the bedroom draperies and threw a thin slice of warmth across the side of the bed where Simon had been sleeping.

She sat up in bed and looked around, memories of the night began returning slowly. Her first feeling was one of pity for Ben. Her second was one of embarrassment for the way she had acted with Simon, literally begging him to stay with her.

There was about an inch of grayish light beneath the bathroom door, and Mariele assumed that Simon was in there dressing, since his clothes had disappeared from the chair where he had laid them out the night before. Slipping into a robe, she went to the kitchen to make coffee, although she was sure Simon would be disappointed with the off-the-shelf brand she used. He had his own exotic blend of beans ground for him at a trendy little shop in the East Village.

Within minutes, the smell of coffee and cinnamon-raisin bagels filled the apartment, but there still had been no sound from the bathroom.

"Simon?" Mariele asked, with her ear close to the door. "Coffee's on." No answer. "Simon, do you need anything?" Silence. "Damn it, Simon, answer me, this isn't funny."

"All right, I'll be out in two or three minutes."

When he finally emerged, looking like death warmed over, Mariele wished he would go home without his coffee, but he docilely followed her to the kitchen and sat down at the table. He looked like an old man, wrinkled and mottled skin hung loose on his bones. His beautiful silvery hair looked thin, and he appeared to be worn out, almost too tired to lift his cup.

"You don't look so good," Mariele said, thinking that was the understatement of the year.

"Just a touch of flu, nothing serious." He forced a smile and took a sip of his coffee. When Mariele offered a toasted bagel, he politely refused it.

"You looked fine last night," she said.

"For God's sake, Mariele, I'm feeling a little under the weather this morning. Try not to make a federal case out of it."

"Sorry. Would you like to stay here and rest today?" she asked. Thankfully, he refused, using the pressure of his work as an excuse to hurry home.

After she watched him climb into a cab in front of the building, she rushed back to the bedroom, stripped the bed, and stuffed everything into the hamper. A little more fuel for her cleaning lady's wild imagination. She hated doing it, but Simon looked so sick. What if he had something more

than a cold or the flu, something contagious?
Something dangerous?

When the bed was made up with fresh linens,
Mariele took a legal pad from her desk and sat
down in the living room. She wanted to write down
everything Ben had said last night, as closely as
she could remember. She didn't even think about
going to work, or of returning the calls from her
few remaining clients.

As she scribbled on the yellow pad, she kept losing the edges of her thoughts. They drifted away
from her, so that every sentence she began trailed
off at the end with a word or two missing. Sometimes she let a squiggle fill in for a word that she
couldn't remember, a word that was snatched out
of her mind by . . .

Graythings everywhere. Pressing down. So many.
If they stole her mind, would she know it? Would
she be aware that she was functioning at half-
power, with lower intelligence? Would the thoughts
that ran through her mind eventually cease to be
her own?

Standing abruptly, Mariele threw the pad across
the room, grabbed her coat, and ran out of the
apartment. As she stepped off the elevator, she
saw a man who looked vaguely familiar walking
away from the building. Once she recognized him
as Dr. Rosenkrantz, she called out his name and
ran to catch up with him.

"Mrs. Hollander? How nice to see you looking
so well."

"Call me Mariele, please, Doctor."

"Only if you will call me Bruce and allow me to drag you along to a lonely luncheon."

"That would be wonderful, Bruce." And it would be. Anything would be better than staying in her apartment with the graythings picking away at her brain.

Bruce Rosenkrantz was one of the most level-headed men Mariele had ever met. Sitting at a table with him, she felt as if they shared a tiny island of calm in the middle of the bustling Manhattan lunch crowd. Diners bumped into their chairs, and waiters lifted heavy trays over their heads, but Mariele felt strangely at peace. When she returned home, she stood in front of the full-length mirror in her bedroom and stared at her gaunt reflection.

"You have been a very sick woman," she said aloud, "but you're going to get better now. You're going to take the first steps on the long road to healing. Ben would want it that way." She waited for the graythings to protest, but they were strangely silent.

The next morning she had her hair cut into a style that mimicked Paula Zahn's, then sat patiently while a chatty young girl filed and painted her nails. When she left the shop, she felt ten times better than she had for weeks.

The next order of business was to sort through the stacks of mail on her desk and to start returning the calls she had ignored. Some of her older clients had dumped her and even didn't want to talk to her now. Others let her know that if they

talked to her again, it would be on their terms and
in their own good time. It was depressing, but she
couldn't blame them for not welcoming her back
with open arms after the way she'd treated them.

There was one unfamiliar name on the answering machine tape, and Mariele almost skipped over
it. The message had been left by a man. His name
was Gene Phillips, and his number was not one
she remembered dialing before. Mariele punched
in the numbers and waited while the phone rang
three times. She was ready to hang up when a
woman's voice answered "Phillipses' residence."

"Hello, this is Mariele Hollander. You left a
message on my machine."

"Oh, Ms. Hollander, I'm so glad you were able
to get back to us. I know how busy you are—you
just finished decorating my cousin's house in
Greenwich last month. But I need some help cre-
ating a perfect room. We'll pay whatever you ask."

Mariele laughed, and felt as if she had taken a
step back into familiar territory.

"Mrs. Phillips, why don't we set up an appointment. I can visit your home, listen to what you
have in mind, and we'll see what we can work out."

"Oh, that would be wonderful. Could you come
today?"

"By coincidence, I've just had a cancellation, so
why not? Give me your address, and I can be on
my way within the next half hour."

The Phillipses' address led Mariele to a building
almost identical to the one she lived in, only
slightly more upscale. A doorman helped her out

of the cab and insisted on carrying her sample
case as far as the elevator, where a uniformed elevator operator took her in charge.

When the car stopped and the doors opened,
Mariele stepped forward and almost collided with
a thin, pale-skinned woman who appeared to be
slightly older than herself.

"I'm Eugenia Phillips," the woman said, extend-
ing her hand.

"Mariele Hollander. You're the Gene, who telephoned me?"

"My husband made the call for me, but I'm
Gene." The woman led Mariele to the door of the
apartment directly across from the elevator and
showed her into a quietly elegant foyer.

"This is lovely," Mariele observed. "I don't believe I've ever been in this building before."

"Carl and I have lived here for fifteen years,"
Gene said, confirming that she was even older than
Mariele had thought. "I thought I'd show you the
room that I want you to do, and then, we'll have
tea afterward while we talk. Is that all right with
you?"

"That would be fine."

Mariele followed Gene through a gray and yellow
living room with wonderful natural light and down
a short hallway.

"Here we are." Gene turned to Mariele and
smiled before she threw open the door to a spacious bedroom. The room was decorated in shades
of green with touches of rose, but the pattern of
color and design had been interrupted. In the cen-

ter of the room stood an ornately carved wooden crib. And in the crib lay a tiny sleeping baby.

"Yours?" Mariele asked in a whisper.

"Yes, my daughter. Laurel is six weeks old today. She's the result of my third pregnancy. The first two ended in miscarriages."

"She's beautiful, and my guess is that you want to remodel this room for her." Still, Mariele couldn't help but wonder why a couple who could obviously afford it had waited until their child was six weeks old before they thought of preparing a room for her.

Gene answered the unasked question. "We were so afraid that I'd miscarry again. We felt that if we made the room into a nursery, something might go wrong again. Even after she was born, we were afraid. But now she's six weeks old and healthy as a little horse, and we want to make this room over for her. We want a room she can enjoy now and ten years from now. A room she can grow up in. I hope you'll help me do that. Carl and I both loved what you did for my cousin."

Mariele walked over to the crib and looked down at the sleeping child. She was beautiful, with pale white skin and wisps of yellow hair on her perfectly shaped head. Her tiny hands were clenched into fists, and her rosebud mouth moved as she drifted through her own private dreamland.

Mariele reached down and gently touched the sleeping baby's hand with her fingertips. It was velvety soft, the softest thing Mariele had ever touched. For a moment, she wanted desperately to lift the child into her arms and press it to her heart.

"Mrs. Hollander?" Gene Phillips's voice cut into Mariele's fantasies.

"I'm sorry. I was just thinking what a lovely child she is. I want very much to do this room for you, Mrs. Phillips."

Over tea and sandwiches, the two women discussed carpeting and curtains and furniture. Gene Phillips reiterated time and time again that money was no object. She and Mariele discovered that they shared a common goal—to create the perfect room for the perfect female child.

Later, Mariele's enthusiasm waned, and she wondered what had come over her in the Phillipses' apartment. It was just a job, like thousands of jobs she'd had previously. She had done rooms for children before, although never on such a lavish scale. The child was lucky, born with a silver spoon in her mouth and with parents who would dote on her every day of her life.

"I may never have a child," Mariele thought, remembering how the little girl had looked lying in the crib, and a cold wave of sadness washed over her. Ben had wanted children, but she had put him off until her career was firmly established. "I should have given Ben a child to carry on his name," she thought now, and a single tear dropped onto one of the drawings she had made to submit to Gene and Carl Phillips.

She tried to call Simon, but the message on his machine said that he was out of town on another of his mysterious business trips. She resigned herself to one more lonely evening, and she pushed her fear of the graythings to the back of her mind.

A grilled cheese and tomato sandwich served as dinner, eaten in front of the television set turned to the evening news. The color on her set was bad, both the news anchor and the weather man looked sickly gray. Mariele switched off the set and finished her sandwich standing in the kitchen. She wanted to leave the apartment, but there was no place to go.

The plans for the Phillipses' nursery should have held her attention for hours, but her concentration was gone. A shower and an early bedtime seemed to be her only recourse. Mariele stripped off her clothes in her bedroom and padded barefoot into the bathroom. She turned on the shower and lathered her body with bath gel. Following her ritual, she ran a brush through her newly cropped hair and gave it a few extra strokes. She was beginning to feel better. Stepping into the shower, closing the glass doors behind her, and throwing her head back to accept the warm water on her face and neck, she felt the tension drain from her body. Her eyes were closed when something cold touched her stomach and wrapped itself around her waist.

She knew what it was, and she had to force herself to open her eyes and face it. Maybe "face it" was the wrong expression. It had no face. It was as tall as she was, with little substance. A slithering gray thing, with arms like tentacles that wrapped themselves around her wet body.

Mariele struggled with the thing that held her, and she pounded at it with her fists. It clung to her and slid easily up and down her body until she was sick and disgusted. Finally, she leaned back against the shower wall and reached down behind her. Scalding hot water pelted the thing and washed it away. A trembling Mariele watched as it was sucked down the drain and disappeared.

thirteen

That night Mariele dreamed, and the dream was of a tiny female child lying in a white crib. She was wearing a long white dress that covered her tiny hands and feet, and only her perfect little face was visible. Mariele put her hand on the child's brow, and the child made a slight movement. "I'm alive," was the message the movement conveyed, and Mariele smiled.

She leaned over the side of the crib and moved her face closer to the child's. Sandy hair and brows, translucent eyelids covering deep blue eyes, pursed lips the color of raspberry sherbet. Mariele's heart swelled with love for the tiny being, and she willed the little girl to wake up so that she could pick her up and hold her.

"Wake up, Allison," she whispered, "wake up and smile for me." But the child slept on, blissfully unaware of Mariele's presence.

Then, suddenly the room turned cold, and the child stirred. Mariele looked around, and saw the graythings sliding up and down the green walls of the oversize nursery. She wanted to cry out for someone to come and save the child, but when she opened her mouth, no sound came. She bent over the crib, determined to grab the child and carry it to safety. But when she lifted it in her arms, she nearly dropped it back to the mattress. The baby had opened her eyes, and they were not the eyes of an infant. They were old beyond their years. They were Ben's eyes, dark, intense, and filled with pain.

Mariele woke with a start and sat up in the bed. The dream had been so real that she looked around for the infant, rearranging the bedclothes in an effort to find it. Then, she realized that she was home in her own bed, not in the nursery she had seen in her dream.

She shuddered, realizing that it was very cold in the apartment. Winter had finally come, and there had been no adjustment in the heat by the building management. She got out of bed and fiddled with the thermostat, but it seemed to be stuck on sixty-two.

The baby will catch cold, she thought, before she could stop herself. Allison will need a warmer room than this if she's going to grow up strong and healthy.

"Allison?" she said aloud. "Where did that come from?" She thought the dream had been inspired by Gene Phillips's beautiful little daughter, but that child's name had been Lauren. No, Laurel, that was it.

Then, she remembered what her subconscious mind had obviously never forgotten. Allison was the name she and Ben had chosen years ago for their own first female child.

Mariele sat down on the edge of the bed and stared at the patterns of frost on the bedroom window. As she watched, the patterns shifted, and gray water ran down the pane and slid across the windowsill. Tiny graythings floated through the air toward her. Even though the bathroom was no safer than the bedroom, she decided to wash her face and brush her teeth.

When she was dressed in warm clothing, she took her briefcase and left the apartment. She had nowhere to go, but even the mean streets of New York City offered more security than the gray walls of her own apartment.

Gene Phillips wanted Mariele to come by and bring some fabric swatches, but Mariele begged off. She agreed to drop off her sketches though, and after stopping off for coffee, she took a cab to their neighborhood. Gene was waiting for her, and Mariele had a hard time getting away from the woman without another visit to the would-be nursery. For some reason that she couldn't explain even to herself, she didn't want to see the baby again, not yet. Her dream of the previous night was still too fresh in her mind. She didn't know what the dream meant, but she feared that maybe her own mind had already been taken over by the graythings, and now, they were going to use her to get the baby.

She left the Phillipses' apartment quickly, and she spent the remainder of the day and evening in a movie theater, watching the same movie over and over.

When she finally arrived home around eleven o'clock, the graythings were everywhere. They were in the brakish water that ran from the faucet in the kitchen and in the toilet when she flushed it. They slithered up and down the walls, silent except for the rasping noise their formless bodies made as they scraped against the wallpaper and against each other.

Mariele knew she would dream again, but there was no way to avoid it. She had to lie down out of sheer exhaustion, and try as she might, she couldn't keep her eyes from closing once she did.

This time she dreamed of a high white hospital bed, a bed of screaming white-hot pain. Everything was white—the sheets, the blankets, the walls, the extended mound of her belly as she strained to deliver her child.

There were no doctors present and no nurses. Only a midwife, stern and impatient with Mariele's fear.

"Push," she commanded.

"I can't," Mariele cried, trying to avoid the onslaught of another terrible contraction.

The midwife slapped her, a solid blow to the side of her face. "You are a weak girl," she said, with disgust. "You do not deserve to have a child."

"Don't say that," Mariele cried. "Please, don't say that."

"Push, push!" the woman commanded again, and this time Mariele pushed until she came close to fainting from the pain. A moment later, she heard the baby crying.

"Good, it is a girl," the midwife said. There was a man's voice then. Mariele couldn't understand his words, but her heart went out to him in his sadness.

There was more to the dream, but Mariele couldn't remember it when she woke up at six A.M., feeling as if she had actually delivered a child during the night. There was pain in her pelvic area, and when she swung her legs over the side of the bed, she found that they were trembling. Her back hurt, too, and she generally felt as if she had been run over by a truck while she slept.

The dream had been vivid, and stranger still, she felt that her morning-after memories were memories of more than just a dream. The more she thought about it, the more she believed that she had actually delivered a child sometime in the past. Otherwise, how would her body be able to know and remember exactly what the pain was like?

It was now November 1995, and Ben had died in October of 1994. That year had been a blur and, granted, there were days, maybe even weeks at a time, that seemed to have slipped away from her. But had she lost enough time to have a baby and then forget about it, maybe due to some trauma she had experienced? It didn't seem very likely.

"This is wild," she told herself. "If you tell anyone that you think you experienced childbirth just because of a realistic dream, they'll put you away."

But the doubt persisted until she knew that she would have to put it to rest. There was one way to find out for sure, and she knew what it was.

"Dr. Rosenkrantz? I'm sorry to bother you, but I was afraid to call, this is a very personal matter."

The doctor had opened the door just a few inches, but now, he swung it wide and pulled Mariele inside his apartment.

"Are you sick?" he asked, laying the back of his hand across her forehead. He had surprisingly small, soft hands for a man his size. Mariele shook her head to indicate that she wasn't physically ill.

"I need to talk to you," she said, as she walked into a living room furnished with bulky black leather couches and chairs.

"Sit, and I'll put the kettle on."

"No, please, I really need to talk now."

He sat down next to her on a long leather sofa and waited for her to begin.

"I know you're going to think this is ridiculous, but I've been having these vivid dreams, and I think I may have had a baby, then erased the pregnancy and the birth from my memory."

"Why would you do that?" Bruce asked calmly, as if this was something he heard every day.

"I don't know. Because of some terrible trauma? Maybe the baby died or something."

"This is very extraordinary, Mariele. Are you sure these dreams of yours are not simply what they appear to be—dreams, pure and simple."

"They're so real," Mariele answered, looking into the doctor's eyes, hoping to convey the strange feelings that were even now coursing through her body.

"There's one way to find out for sure, isn't there?" she asked. "If I ever have delivered a child, wouldn't a doctor be able to tell?"

"A pelvic examination would reveal the truth," Bruce answered carefully. "Is that what you want, do you want me to recommend someone?"

"Can you do it yourself?" Mariele stood and put both hands on the waistband of her slacks.

"You mean here? Now? I'm sure that could appear to be very unethical. I can recommend you to a good friend of mine who will be the soul of discretion should there be a need for it."

"Here and now, Bruce, please. I feel as if I'm losing my mind. I can't call a stranger and make an appointment. I can't fill out forms and make small talk with nurses while I wait to find out if the things I dreamed last night are really memories. Can you try to understand that and help me?"

"I want to help you, Mariele, but how do I know . . . I don't know you very well, after all."

A smile broke out on Mariele's face, and she laughed without humor. "What's the matter, Bruce, do you think I'm setting you up? Do you think a reporter from 'Hard Copy' is going to burst through the door as soon as I take my pants down?"

"No, no, of course not, but this is my home,

Mariele. I don't have the equipment here to do a pelvic."

"You have a table," Mariele said, striding into the kitchen and pointing to the black Formica-topped table in the center of the room.

Bruce followed her and stopped just inside the kitchen door. "You're serious, aren't you?"

"Quite."

"This is completely against my better judgment." He shrugged his wide shoulders and stared past her for a few seconds before he met her eyes. "All right," he said. "Give me a minute to set up here. There's a robe on the back of the bathroom door. Slip off everything from the waist down and put it on."

Mariele went through the motions in a daze and returned to the kitchen quickly before she had a chance to come to her senses and change her mind. Bruce was waiting for her, the table swathed in clean white sheets.

"You're sure you want to do this?"

She nodded and he helped her climb onto the table. A few minutes of discomfort, and it was all over. The doctor was completely professional, in spite of the strange circumstances, so there was little cause for embarrassment.

"Well?" she asked, when he turned away to remove his gloves.

"Get dressed first."

She came back to the kitchen and found the sheets and the doctor's tools gone. He was setting the table with delicate china and spoons.

"Tea," he said, indicating the pot of boiling water. "I think we both need it." When she sat down at the table, he handed her a loaf of bread, a butter knife, and a jar of peanut butter. "Sandwich?"

Mariele laughed and started to shake her head, then her stomach rumbled, and she remembered that she had skipped breakfast.

"I don't remember the last time I ate," she said, and covered two slices of white bread with a generous amount of Skippy. Bruce let her eat half of the sandwich before he told her of his findings.

"Mariele, something strange is happening in your life. The day I met you something you couldn't explain had happened to you, and again, the day I took you out to lunch. Now, today, you tell me that you dreamed about giving birth to a child, even though you are not consciously aware of ever having been pregnant."

"Go on."

"According to your body, you did give birth to a child."

"When?" The room was whirling around Mariele, and the peanut butter threatened to come up. That was the only question she could think of to ask. "When?"

"I can't tell. No one could tell. There are scars where old tears have healed. There are other signs."

"No mistake?"

"No mistake. Somewhere in the world there is a child who came from your womb."

"What if that child died?"

"There would be a death certificate."

"What if she's still alive and someone took her from me?"

"There should still be a record of the birth. Sit down, Mariele, I can't let you leave here like this." The doctor brought a box of tissues from the counter and handed her a large wad of them. Only then did she realize that she was crying.

fourteen

Bruce was kind enough to use his clout to assist Mariele in cutting through the red tape at the Bureau of Vital Statistics. If it hadn't been for him, it would have taken her days, or possibly weeks, to fill out all the necessary forms, submit them with the proscribed fees and wait for them to be processed.

By the end of the afternoon, she knew that there was no birth certificate for a baby girl Hollander and, more importantly, no death certificate. Of course, that didn't prove much. The baby could have been born outside of the city, or even in another state. Bruce was already busy pulling strings to cover that possibility.

Mariele refused the doctor's offer of dinner and also his offer to share a cab back to their apartment building. She started walking aimlessly, only later realizing that she was heading in the direction of Simon's apartment. She liked the doctor and respected him, but she couldn't share her feelings with him the way she could with Simon.

"Be home," she whispered when she was still dozens of blocks away. "Be home, Simon."

The walk took her hours, and the sky was pitch

black when she arrived on the street where Simon lived. Her heart sunk when she discovered that there were no lights on in his apartment. She sat down on the stoop, depressed and exhausted. The next thing she knew, someone was shaking her by the shoulders and calling her name. She looked up into Simon's face.

"Mariele, what in the world are you doing out here? Are you out of your mind? It's cold as hell, and this isn't the safest place in the world to camp out. Thank God one of my neighbors recognized you."

When she stared at him blankly, Simon paced in front of her and said, "Like yeah, man, it's your old lady, the one who's always down here bustin' ya, man." He did a wonderful job of imitating one of the tough punks who owned the neighborhood streets, and Mariele laughed despite her discomfort.

"Where are my wits?" Simon wondered aloud. "Come inside before you get sick sitting out here in twenty-five degree weather."

Mariele didn't realize that she was freezing until she walked into the warm apartment and started to thaw out, which was a painful process. Although Simon made his usual pot of tea and treated her hospitably, she immediately noticed a certain reticence about him. When she told him about her dreams, he pulled back even further, saying that he never had put much stock in dreams, which wasn't what he had indicated before.

The last straw was Mariele's recounting of Bruce's examination. Simon had been pacing nervously;

now, he stopped in front of her chair and leaned over her. She tried to press herself into the back of the chair to get away from him, but there was nowhere to go.

Simon's voice was loud and harsh, so unlike him that it was almost as if another entity spoke through him.

"You're acting like a whore!" he screamed. "What decent woman would go to a man's apartment and demand that he give her an examination of that kind? Isn't it the law that a nurse has to be present, even if it's done in a doctor's office? He could go to jail for touching you like that, and I might be the one to put him there."

"Simon, you're scaring me," Mariele whispered, pushing on his chest. He straightened but remained standing over her chair, threatening her with his eyes and the wild expression on his face.

"You're being irrational," she continued, gaining more nerve to stand up to him. "First of all, you don't own me, so you can't dictate what I do. Secondly, I'm trying to explain how I feel, but you only listen to what you want to hear. I'm sorry I came here at all. For some mistaken reason, I thought you were my friend."

"I'm trying to be rational, Mariele, but it isn't easy. This dream of yours wasn't a memory of something that really happened, at least not in this lifetime. I've dealt with things like this before, and there are several possible explanations. I wish you had thought to contact me before you went to see this so-called doctor. By the way, did you think to

check out his credentials before you laid yourself
out on his kitchen table?"

"Simon, please . . ."

He shrugged and turned away, and the thought
struck Mariele that he must care for her more than
he had let on before. The thought of her naked
before Bruce was obviously driving Simon crazy.

"As I was saying, there are explanations. This
could be the memory of an experience from another lifetime. You said there was no hospital
equipment involved, no doctors, only a midwife.
Have you ever been regressed?"

"No."

"So, you don't know precisely how any of your
previous lifetimes ended? Maybe this is the explanation for one of them, possibly the most recent.
Maybe you died in childbirth."

"I didn't die after the birth of the baby, Simon.
In one of the dreams, she was lying in a crib, and
I was watching her sleep."

"That probably wasn't a true memory of your
own experience."

"Then, what was it?" Mariele asked impatiently.

"A short-term memory from your visit to that
woman, Gene?"

"Gene Phillips."

"Yes. You said that the room in the dream
looked like the room where you saw their baby."

"I don't think that explains it, Simon, it wasn't
even the same baby. I'm sorry, but I don't think it
was a past-life experience, and I don't think it was
the Phillipses' baby in the dream, although it

might have been their baby who brought back the memory."

"Very well," Simon said petulantly, "if you don't want to believe me, I can't help you, can I?"

"Give me a chance to think about this, okay? You've just hit me with something very heavy. Surely, you can't expect me to believe it without even taking time to think about it?"

"You're right. You must be worn out. Come and lie down with me."

He walked her to the bedroom, supporting her, treating her as if she was an invalid. When her head touched the pillow, the room swam around her. It swirled faster and faster until it finally disappeared. When she woke up, the clock said that it was noon, and Simon was gone. She had gotten through a night without dreaming, and a night without the graythings. Her attitude changed to the point where it was almost upbeat.

On the way home from Simon's apartment, Mariele told herself that she had to put Ben, the graythings, and the Thanatological Society out of her mind if she wanted to survive with her sanity intact. No more thoughts of Dwago, she told herself. And no more dreams. Especially, no more dreams.

It was time to start dating again, and that didn't mean Simon. Join a dating service, she told herself, put an ad in the personals, say yes to the next nice young man who asks you to a movie. Get your life back in gear.

The day was bright and clear, and she almost

felt as if she had driven away the graythings with her improved mood. There were no shadows in the apartment today, no gray raindrops sliding down the windows.

Mariele decided that it was a good day to start cleaning out some closets, a chore she hadn't managed to do since before Ben's death. She knew there were still boxes of his books in the hall closet, books that could be donated to the library in his name. And there was clothing that could be given to a homeless shelter. Ben would like that. She had hung onto his things long enough. Now, it was time to part with them.

The bedroom closet was her first choice, since that was where he had kept most of his clothing. She opened his side of the closet, pushed the folding doors to one side, and faced Ben's possessions for the first time in months. She started to remove clothing from the closet and laid it out on the bed. Later, she would call downstairs and ask one of the doormen to bring up a few boxes so that she could pack the clothing, the books, and whatever else she found before she changed her mind about parting with it.

She worked fast, and soon, the bed was piled high. There were three suits, a topcoat, a London Fog, and several jackets on hangers. From the shelves above, she removed Dockers and jeans and dozens of shirts and sweaters. They were all neatly folded and stacked on the bed.

Mariele decided to remove the shoes from the closet floor before she made the call for the boxes.

That way, even if she did no more today, she would feel that she'd accomplished something. Ben's side of the closet would be bare, ready to be dusted and prepared for her own use.

Getting down on her knees, she reached for a pair of boots she had seen in the rear of the closet. Somehow, she lost her balance and fell forward. Her outstretched hand struck the back wall of the closet, and it moved.

"Great construction," she noted, then pushed on the wall to test its strength. The panel felt as if it was made of cardboard. Mariele climbed into the closet and looked more closely at its construction. The wall on Ben's side was a good six or eight inches off from the wall on her side. After going to the kitchen for a screwdriver, she was able to remove the fake wall easily and put it aside.

She found a black leather-bound book that was filled with pages written in Ben's spidery handwriting, and Mariele felt sure that it would satisfy her curiosity about the strange society that had counted her husband as a member.

There was nothing else in Ben's private little cubicle, at least, nothing important. Sheets. There were what appeared to be several white bedsheets crumpled into balls in the far corner of the space. That was curious, but not of any consequence. Mariele pulled them out, stood, and shook out one of them. She dropped it to the floor, as if it had been filled with snakes. The sheet was covered with splotches of dried blood.

It took only seconds to figure out where the

sheets had come from. She knew without a doubt
that her baby had been born here, in this apartment, while Ben was still alive, and that it was he
who had hidden the sheets in the secret compartment in his closet. She knew it even before she
clutched at her stomach and fell onto the bed, remembering.

There was no hospital bed, as she had pictured
in her dream. The birth had taken place right here
in her own bedroom, on the very bed upon which
she now had fallen. As she watched, a man lifted
her, while someone else slid a thick, spongy pad
beneath her. That had added height to the bed,
so that in her delirium she had thought it was a
hospital bed.

The man, who had lifted her, placed her gently
back in the bed and leaned down to kiss her cheek.
It was Ben, her very own Ben, the man who had
longed so for a child of his own. He was weeping,
telling her that he loved her, saying that it soon
would be over. She had no sympathy for him now.
She only knew that her child had been born while
he was still alive and that he had taken it away
from her.

The pictures that played in front of Mariele's eyes
now were much more vivid than any dream. She was
reliving the torment of childbirth, reexperiencing
the pain she had suffered that day, both physical and
mental.

The hands of the midwife were rough, and her
voice was unsympathetic. "You are a spoiled, pam-
pered girl," she said, with a thick accent. Some-

thing about her voice caused Mariele to look up into her face. She had not been startled then, but she was now. She jumped up from the bed and moved quickly away from it, as if it would capture her and hold her prisoner to the pain she had once felt there. But she could still see the pictures. There were three other people in the room besides herself—Ben, Dwago, and the midwife, Simon's mother Valda. So, she had been right to have a twinge of suspicion that Simon was involved. She remembered how she had asked Dwago, "Who sent you last night, Simon?" and then believed that he had not, only because she so badly wanted to believe in his innocence. Because she needed someone on her side, because it was so hard to be completely alone in the world.

Mariele's head swam. She wondered if Valda was really Simon's mother, and how they were involved with Dwago. If Simon knew Dwago, then he had been lying to her consistently. And why would Valda deliver her baby, help steal it away from her, and then call Mariele to her bedside when she was dying?

Mariele was frightened, but she was angry, too. More angry than she ever had been in her entire life. She vowed that she would find her baby some-how and get it back—if it was the last thing she ever did.

As she dialed Simon's number, her hands shook with the rage that was coursing through her body. What she would say to him when he answered was unclear. She tried to decide on a course of action, but she couldn't think rationally. She wanted to know why he had deceived her, and she wanted to know where her baby was now. She was going to give him a chance to make it right before she turned him in to the police.

The phone rang and rang, and Simon didn't pick up. He had obviously forgotten to turn on the answering machine, or maybe, he sometimes left it off on purpose. Mariele had no doubt that the only man she had trusted since Ben's death was a very devious man. But Simon was no more devious than Ben. Ben had deceived her. Ben had taken her baby. She wanted to scream at him until her voice was gone. She hated him, and she wanted to find a way to get back at him. How, she wondered, do you take revenge on a dead man?

fifteen

To Mariele's surprise, the International Thanatological Society had a listing in the white pages of the Manhattan phone directory. She punched the numbers into her phone, still trembling with anger. An answering machine picked up the call, and a cold, robotic voice urged the caller to leave a message.

Mariele was tempted to throw the phone across the room, but she gritted her teeth and waited for the beep. Then, she let out the breath she had been holding and left her message.

"Dwago, this is Mariele Hollander. I know. I know about the baby, and I want you to tell me what you did with her. You have one hour to call me back. If you don't, I'll call the police and tell them everything I know."

She slammed down the receiver and sat on a chair in the kitchen, where she had made the call, to wait for the phone to ring.

Either the phone was in Dwago's apartment or the society's communication system was damn good. Mariele's phone rang exactly eleven minutes after she had placed the call to him. He didn't sound scared, as she had hoped he would. He was slightly amused, if anything, and that made her even more angry.

"You've lost your control over me, Dwago," she said, exercising all the self-control she could muster. "I know that Simon is one of you, and I know about Valda."

"Mariele, you'd better understand that Ben was in on everything that happened. In fact, almost all of it was his idea."

"Screw Ben," she screamed. "I'm onto him, too. And whoever the hell's been calling me from New Jersey . . ." That idea came to her out of the blue, and Mariele went with it. "Tell them to let me alone, because if I find out who they are—"

"Someone's been calling you? From Fort Lee?"

"From New Jersey, that's all I know." But Dwago had slipped, and now, Mariele had a clue that the house they had taken her to just might be in Fort Lee. She screamed a little longer before she agreed to let Dwago come over to her apartment and tell her everything.

Halfway across the George Washington Bridge on her way to Fort Lee, she laughed aloud, picturing Dwago frantically pounding on the door to her apartment, demanding entrance. Pulling over to the side of the road, she opened the glove compartment and extracted a map of New Jersey. She tried to figure out what route Dwago had taken the night he took her to the house where the meeting was held, but she couldn't be sure of which streets they had taken. She figured that the best thing to do was to drive through the town of 32,000 inhabitants, cruising up and down the streets until she recognized the house. One hell of a long shot, but what else could she do? If she was lucky enough to find the house, what she would do then was a mystery.

As she entered the town of Fort Lee, night fell suddenly, as quickly as if someone had pulled down a curtain to shut out the light. It had been a cold day, and now, it turned damp, as well. Icy puddles formed on the roads, and driving became hazardous. Mariele's car slid around a corner and almost slammed into a parked truck before she regained control.

Water dripped down the windshield so heavily that the wipers were ineffectual. Parked by the curb on a side street, Mariele tried to clean the car windows with paper towels, but that didn't work either. The paper stuck to the windows and froze there as the cold water ran over it in sheets.

Back in the car, she rubbed her hands together and massaged her fingers in an attempt to bring feeling back to them. The temperature was surely below zero, and water was pouring from the sky, a deluge of icy slush that froze everything in sight. She turned on the radio, hoping to hear a news report about the ice storm, but the airways were filled with static.

"I'm in the Twilight Zone," she said aloud, as she pulled back onto the slippery roadway.

Everyone else in the world seemed to have been forewarned about the bad weather. There were no cars on the roads and no pedestrians in sight. On her drive through the city, Mariele saw no buses, no police cars, no commuters hurrying home from work. Everyone in the small New Jersey town of Fort Lee seemed to be safely in their homes, tucked in for the night. Everyone but Mariele Hollander, who was determined to forge on until she found the house of evil that had swallowed up her husband and her baby daughter.

Visibility was near zero and, as if that wasn't enough, the car seemed to be exhibiting mechanical problems. It stalled out several times, and each time, it became harder for Mariele to get it started again. In the suburbs of the town, the streets were wider and the houses farther apart. Some of them looked like mini-estates, and she thought this was surely the neighborhood where the mystery house was located. Still, she shuddered thinking about the prospect of being stranded out here if the car broke down. Most of the houses looked dark and deserted, while those with lights on looked cold and unapproachable. These were not the kind of doors you knocked on to ask for help on a night like this.

She was wondering how much more time she should spend looking for the house before she gave up and returned to her warm apartment when she saw it. It was the first English Tudor style house she'd seen all evening, the most imposing house on a street of very expensive real estate.

She turned the wheel to the left and pulled into

the driveway and cut the motor. The gray rain fell so heavily that it was questionable whether or not she would be able to make it to the house. She took a deep breath and decided to try it. The car door was grabbed out of her hands by the wind, riffled back and forth as if it was a sheet of paper, then slammed hard. Mariele wasn't able to move fast enough, and the door hit her left elbow with a hard blow. She said a few choice words, then slid over to the passenger side of the car. That door was slightly easier to open, and she was more aware of what to expect. When the wind caught the door and pulled it away from her, she moved fast and slid out into the storm before the door could be used as a weapon and slammed into her body.

Standing in the pelting rain was hard; walking in it was impossible. With every step Mariele took, the wind pushed her back two steps. Finally, she fell to her knees and crawled to the front door of the house.

By the time she reached the house, she was covered in mud and drenched to the skin. She hadn't been prepared for the rain, so her raincoat was hanging safe and dry in her closet at home. The cloth coat that she wore was now a piece of heavy, matted wool. Her hair clung to her head and dripped water onto her shoulders. She knew this, but she was still unprepared for the sight of her own reflection in a dark window on the left side of the house. She started, then had to laugh when she realized that she had been frightened by her own face in the glass.

The porch was wide, made of wood, and the floor was probably squeaky. To tiptoe across it in waterlogged shoes would probably not be possible. Mariele slid off her pumps and slipped one into each pocket of her coat. Her toes had been cold before. Now, they felt like frozen clumps of ice affixed to the ends of her feet. She shivered and put one foot in front of the other carefully until she stood before the imposing front door.

If the door was locked, she had no clue as to what she would do next, but luckily for her, it swung open when she turned the knob. Probably because so many people come and go here all the time, she reasoned. But where were all those people now? The big house was silent and dark except for the single light in the right front window.

Mariele tried to find her way down the same corridors she had walked with Dwago a month ago, but the house looked different tonight. It's the darkness, she reassured herself, and the storm outside.

After a few wrong turns, she found the room where the meeting had been held. Books lined the walls, and the room was dominated by a long, polished wooden table where the members had been seated. There was a low-watt bulb burning in a desk lamp on one end of the table that made it easy to find the projection screen television and the video tapes stored in the cabinet beneath it.

The tape from July 17 was clearly marked "Birth," and Mariele's hand was surprisingly steady as she loaded the cassette into the machine and pushed the play button. It had happened exactly as she remembered it—the labor, the birth, the fragile little girl child lying in the crib.

What had happened after that was not in her memory, most of it never had been. After that one glimpse of the child, she had been dragged away by Dwago and a man she didn't recognize. But after she was gone, the camera had kept rolling.

Everything in the room looked as if it was underwater. The camera lens was wet, dripping with something thick and gray. Ben's curly dark hair was plastered to his head, his shirt wet enough to wring out. The baby herself looked as if she had been given a bath with her clothes on.

The room and its furnishings turned gray, then grayer, then grayer still. Ben became an old man before Mariele's eyes, the skin under his eyes wrinkling and bagging, his dark hair losing its color.

Mariele didn't scream when she saw something gray drop from the ceiling and float across the room toward the baby's crib. She didn't move now, as Ben hadn't moved then. He let the thing enter the crib with his only child and cover the baby with slimy gray matter. When it slithered away, the mattress was gray and wet. The baby was gone. When the camera zoomed in on Ben's face, he had aged at least forty years.

"Allison," Mariele whispered, turning away from the television and sinking into a chair beside the table. She wanted to cry, but the shock was too great. She felt numb, not frightened or angry with Ben, or sick at the injustice of what had happened to her child. She knew that would come later. Right now, she was just numb.

"Mariele Hollander, you are a stupid woman." The voice came from the doorway and without turning around to look, Mariele knew that it belonged to Dwago.

"And you are a murderer," she said, beginning to feel the pain of her grief.

"That title belongs to your precious Ben. It was his idea to offer them the baby. But he had good intentions, he did it for you. Do you want to know what really happened?"

She nodded her head and waited, sure that Dwago's ego would force him to tell her what he knew. She was right.

"When you got pregnant, it was too late. Ben had already pledged his suicide and the graythings were waiting for him. They waited a long time while he made his preparations, and you could say they were disappointed when Ben discovered he had something to live for. If they couldn't have his soul, they were going to take yours. It was either you or the baby. Or Ben, of course. Since he'd already decided that he didn't want to die, that narrowed the choice. He said it really wasn't a choice. He loved you that much.

"Ironic, isn't it? After they took the baby away, he couldn't live with himself, so he committed suicide after all."

"By this time tomorrow, you'll be in jail," Mariele said, still without looking at Dwago. "I'll tell them everything I know, and what I don't know, I'll make up."

Dwago laughed, and the sound turned Mariele's stomach. "It won't do you any good. By tomorrow morning, there'll be a nice upper-class couple living here with two snotty teenage kids. The neighbors will swear they've been here for years. The police will think you're crazy."

"And what about the baby? Babies don't just disappear."

"No, they don't. My guess would be that you'll be charged with murdering your own child before it's all over. What do they call it? Infanticide or something?"

Mariele finally turned to look at Dwago's face. What she saw there made her wonder how she ever had let him touch her. There was little doubt that he was thoroughly enjoying the pain he was inflicting. "Why are you doing this to me?"

"Ben brought you into it. You mean nothing to me, one way or the other. The sex wasn't even that good."

"You're a lousy bastard!"

"So I've been told. Now, get out of here before I forget that Ben and I were friends."

Dwago roughly escorted Mariele to the front door and literally shoved her out onto the porch. The boards were slippery, and she barely caught her balance at the edge of the steps. Her shoes were still in her pockets, but she was afraid to stop long enough to put them on. As she stumbled down the steps, Dwago laughed behind her, then slammed the door. She heard the lock slide into place, and she realized what a fool she was for not knowing that he had set her up. She should have known that he would be there waiting for her.

At least, the freezing rain had stopped, and the sky was clear, although the temperature felt as if it were well below zero.

On the drive back across the George Washington Bridge, Mariele let the tears well up in her eyes, then overflow down her cheeks. Allison had been a reality, but she had only lived for a short time before her precious life was snuffed out. The graythings had taken her, but it was her own father who had let them do it.

Could this actually have happened, or was Mariele losing her mind? Maybe she had gone crazy when Ben died, and all the awful things that happened during the past several months had taken place in her own sick mind? Was it possible that even Dwago was a product of her imagination? "No!" she said aloud, "it is not possible. I have never been sick enough to create a monster like Dwago."

As she neared home, she realized that she had until that moment forgotten about the black note-book Ben had left in the back of his closet with the sheets. She stepped on the gas, and the car sped forward. If there were graythings waiting for her in the apartment, she didn't care. As soon as she settled things with Simon, it wouldn't matter anymore. She would be ready to go with them.

sixteen

Joe, the flirty young doorman, told Mariele that a man had been there looking for her a couple of hours earlier.

"He was real agitated, Mrs. Hollander, wringing his hands, pacing back and forth. Acted like he needed to see you in the worst way."

"Do you remember what he looked like?" she asked, wondering if the young doorman's words were suggestive, or if she was simply reading too much into them.

"Couldn't forget him. Pasty white face, silvery hair. Looked like he just stepped off a Dracula set or something."

"Thank you for remembering to tell me," she said, thankful that the elevator had come while he was busy describing Simon. She made a mental note to tip the man the next time she passed through the lobby. They always said it wasn't necessary, but she knew it couldn't hurt. Anyway, she didn't want the doorman to think that he was doing her any favors.

At least, now, she knew that Simon was in town and that she'd be able to reach him later, when she was ready to talk to him. She wasn't in a hurry. Maybe it would do him good to stew for a little while, especially since he seemed to be so anxious to get in touch with her.

The door to her apartment was hard to open. It stuck, as if it were warped, swollen with dampness. Inside, the air was humid, and Mariele envisioned impending thunderstorms. But the skies over Manhattan were clear, and she knew that the storm she had witnessed in Fort Lee would not have been recorded by the meteorologists with all their sophisticated equipment.

She threw her coat down on the couch and started back to the kitchen to make tea. Then, she heard the beep of the answering machine and decided to take care of that first. She instinctively knew that the message was from Simon even before she pushed the button to activate the machine.

"Mariele, what in the hell are you doing? If you wanted to know about the baby, why didn't you ask me? Dwago is mad as hell, and in the foul mood he's in, he's liable to kill you. Don't go over there. Do you hear me? Don't go to Fort Lee!"

"Too late, Simon," Mariele answered the machine. "It's too late for all of us, Simon, but I have a feeling that you're not going to stop struggling until the bitter end, are you?"

The notebook was where she had left it, but it wouldn't have surprised her if it was missing. Dwago and Simon and how many others had been watching her? Valda? Was the kindly old woman who had started this whole mess really Simon's mother, or just another member of the great society of suicide worshippers? And did it really matter who or what she was? She had been part of the deception, a member of the killing team.

Mariele took the notebook to the kitchen, holding it out in front of her to avoid too much contact with it. It was a kind of daybook with loose-leaf pages for each day of the year. But Ben had used it as a diary without paying much attention to the dates. He had started writing on July 7 and continued through to the middle of October, without so much as a paragraph to separate his thoughts, just a new date now and then to show that time was passing. Until October 16. That's where it ended, the last entry in the book.

"Mariele," it began, "if you are reading these words . . ." That was as far as she got before her eyes filled up with tears. She put her hands out in front of her and pushed at the air, then brought them back to wipe her eyes. She had imagined for a moment that she was in a swimming pool, in a hole filling rapidly with slimy gray water. The image overtook her again, and she fought to climb above the surface. The water level was rising quickly, and soon, her head would be underwater.

"Help me!" she screamed, when she broke the surface. "Can't breathe! Help me!" The water slapped at her face and tugged at her hair with a power straight from hell. Or worse, straight from her childhood fear of the swimming hole on her grandparents' farm. She had feared and hated the feel of the slippery mud under her feet and the murky brown water that fought to push its way into her mouth and nose. How could she have forgotten her fear of that place for so many years? How had she been able to suppress it so successfully? Now, it came back in full force, carrying her back to that place where she had fought to maintain her childhood dignity in the face of such awful fear.

Escape! something shouted in her head, and she ran from the kitchen as if her life depended on it. She knew the room wasn't filling up with water. Her mind knew it, but her instincts of self-preservation protested that knowledge. It had been so real.

With a towel folded over her face for protection, she slipped back into the kitchen several minutes later and grabbed the book from the table. It was wet. As soaking wet as if it had sunk to the bottom of a pool of gray water and laid there for a long, long time. Mariele held it up to the strong light of a lamp in the living room and tried to make out the rest of the first page. "Mariele, if you are reading these words, it will be because Bruce told you where to find this book. I have hidden it because it may never be necessary for you to know the entire truth."

"Oh, Ben, for God's sake, what have you done?" She slammed the book shut and threw it across the room, where it missed the sofa and fell onto the carpet with a wet "plop." It wasn't until the book was out of her hands that she became fully aware of what she had read: ". . . it will be because Bruce told you where to find this book."

Bruce! Her dear new friend Bruce was one of them. Or, at least, that's how it sounded. Otherwise, why would Ben entrust Bruce with his confession, which is what she expected the book to be?

Mariele started across the room to retrieve the book, but she only made it halfway there. When she reached the table in front of the couch, she dropped to her knees and laid her head in her hands. Her forehead was dripping, and her hair was knotted and tangled with something that emitted a nasty odor when she pulled a few strands of hair across her face. She looked down at her hands, which were trembling, and noticed that her skin was gray and wrinkled, as if she had been underwater for a long time.

No one had to tell her that the graythings were getting bolder by the minute. They were taking over her body and starting to work on her mind. She had fallen to her knees because she had lost her equilibrium, but she had stayed there because she momentarily had forgotten the book and her desire to have it back.

When she did remember, she moved swiftly, following through on the thought before they had a chance to grab it away from her. The book was badly damaged and using her hair dryer to dry out the pages did little good. It was obvious that large sections of Ben's writing were gone and were not recoverable. But there were some passages that were still readable, and it was on those that Mariele concentrated.

By the time I learned about the graythings, it was too late. At first, I thought they were a grown-up's version of the boogeyman, something made up to fill in the empty spaces between heaven and hell in our imaginations. I didn't know then how close I came to the truth. But they aren't something out of man's imagination. They're real, and I have committed to them. Nothing that has happened in my life has prepared me for the terror that I know awaits me after death.

There is a purgatory, Mariele, a place where there is neither the glory of heaven nor the everlasting fire and brimstone of hell. There is a place filled with the graythings, which are horrible beyond words. And the most horrible thing of all is that someday I will become one of them.

I know you won't be able to understand why I can't just back out now and continue to live. Trust me when I tell you that it's too late. The world isn't big enough to run from them. Wherever I would go, they would follow me, pecking at the edges of my soul. Anyway, how could I face you every morning with the knowledge that I gave them your only child. Our child.

Mariele closed the book and ran out of the apartment, not stopping to shut her apartment door behind her. The graythings were there, and soon, they would start pecking away at *her* soul, if they hadn't started already. A burglar would not be very high on her list of people to fear after dealing with them.

It took a long time for the elevator to arrive at her floor, and she paced up and down while she waited, trying to form in her mind the questions she would ask Bruce. She had truly thought of him as a friend, and it was hard facing the fact that he was part of the group who had stolen away from her both her husband and her child.

When the elevator doors finally opened on her floor, Mariele stepped inside and pressed the number five. The elevator started with a thump, lurched, and plummeted downward as if it was a missile aimed at the concrete floor of the basement far below. She closed her eyes and waited for the crash, but when the car stopped, the doors opened onto the fifth floor.

No one came to the door, although she rang Bruce's bell a dozen times and called out his name over and over. Determined not to give up, she turned the doorknob and tried to enter his apartment. The door was unlocked, but pushing on it, she met with strong resistance. Then, suddenly the door was jerked open, pulling Mariele into the entryway. She caught her balance and found herself staring into Bruce's sad brown eyes.

"Why didn't you answer the door?" she asked, angry and breathless.

"I was in the bathroom," he answered shortly, refusing to meet her eyes.

"I realize that you probably don't want to talk to me."

"It's not that I mind talking, Mariele, but I think you've already made your decision about what to believe."

"Are you saying that I shouldn't believe in the graythings?"

"They're in the mind of the believer," Bruce answered solemnly. "If you stop acknowledging them, they'll go away and let you alone."

"That isn't true. Ben tried to get them out of his mind after he found out what they were, but it was too late."

"Ben!" Bruce said, dismissing her husband with a wave of his hand. "Ben didn't know what he wanted. He never did. He romanced death the way other men romance a beautiful woman. He courted suicide and welcomed the graythings into his life, knowing full well that he was setting you up as a victim."

"Are you saying that Ben didn't love me?"

"There are different degrees of love," Bruce mumbled, still hiding his eyes from Mariele's scrutiny. "Ben wanted the adventure of it, even if it meant the end of his life."

"How did you know Ben? Where did you meet him?"

"We met right here in the building, shortly after you married and moved in. We ran into each other in the lobby several times when we came in late at night. Once or twice, we happened to be going out for Chinese at the same time and we walked over to the restaurant together. When Ben decided to join the Thanatologians, he found that I was already a member. It went on from there."

"Tell me this, if you're a long-term member of the society, why are you still alive?"

"Because I haven't yet pledged my self-destruction."

"I never would have suspected you to be one of them. I thought you were my friend."

"I am your friend, that has nothing to do with them."

"Oh, yes, it does. I know about the baby. If I decide to press charges, you'll lose your license." Mariele turned away, but Bruce grabbed her arm and prevented her from leaving.

"You found Ben's book?" he asked.

"Yes, I found the book."

"I asked him not to mention my name."

"I guess my husband just couldn't be trusted."

Mariele pulled her arm free and went back to her own apartment. She knew that Bruce was hurt and that he needed to talk, but she didn't care. No one seemed to be interested in what she needed.

Back upstairs, the walls were sweating and the carpet squished under her feet. She wanted a shower, but the bathroom was full of moisture, a slimy gray moisture that she knew couldn't get her clean. They were taking over her body, insinuating themselves into her pores and into every crevice where they could gain entrance. There was no sense in trying to run, because she was sure it was too late to escape them. She almost had grown used to having them share the apartment with her. But now, she could feel them in her mind, slowing down her thought processes, filling her brain with alien thoughts, and making her question her own sanity.

She put her hands up to her temples and applied pressure until the pain was unbearable, but the graythings stayed where they were, their tentacles tightly wrapped around her brain.

seventeen

Sometime during the night, Bruce came up and pounded on the apartment door. Mariele had no idea what time it was, and she ignored his hammering for several minutes before she shouted for him to go away and let her alone.

"I have to talk to you," he yelled back. "Please, Mariele, open the door." But she had fallen back into the dreamlike trance from which he had awakened her, and she found it impossible to rouse herself from her lethargy to walk to the door and let him into the apartment.

She was reliving the first days of her marriage to Ben, the one time of her life when everything had been perfect, when she could have wished for nothing more. Her handsome husband's touch had been like fire on her skin, and she could find no imperfections in the way he dressed, or walked, or talked, or made love to her.

One thing she had loved about Ben from the start was his intelligence. He was a thinking man, and his thoughts ranged across a wide variety of subjects. He was equally interested in the wonder that surrounded the birth of man as he was in the reasons why every man must die.

"If I die first," he said, in her dream, "I'm going to come back and tell you what it's like out there."

"Oh, you are," the dreaming Mariele answered. "Does that mean you're going to sugarcoat it if it's bad?"

"By the time we die," he promised, "we'll be so full of love that we'll float straight up to heaven."

"Both of us?"

"Both of us."

"Promise?"

"I promise. But if there are complications, I'll let you know, so that you'll be prepared."

"You're half-serious, aren't you?" she asked, looking into his solemn dark eyes.

"I am completely serious, my love," he answered, then he touched her lips with his.

Something tugged at her consciousness, but Mariele didn't want to leave the dream. It had been so long since Ben had kissed her, so long since she'd felt his arms around her. She had almost forgotten how wonderful it felt to be touched by him. She had forgotten what romance was like, how wondrous it was to be in love.

"If I could just stay here forever," she murmured, "I would choose never to wake up again. I want to stay here with you, Ben. Please, let me stay here with you." But Ben was pushing her away, and whatever was nibbling at the corners of her dream wouldn't stop. In another moment, she was wide awake, and Ben was gone.

With a sudden jolt of fear, Mariele realized that the dream might not have been what it appeared to be. She had thought at first that it was a memory of the past, but now that she was awake, she didn't remember ever having that exact conversation with Ben. Still, it could have been an ordinary dream, a product of her subconscious mind, but Mariele didn't think so. Ben's arms had felt so real, he had kissed her with such passion, almost as if he knew it was going to be his last chance to taste her lips.

"Ben, were you really here?" she asked, and the electricity in the air told her that he had been. "I was so angry with you last night," she said aloud. "Is that why you came? Were you trying to warn me about the graythings again, even though it's too late for us?"

The sky outside the bedroom windows was pitch-black, and the clock on her bedside table said that it was only four A.M. "Why couldn't I have stayed in the dream?" she asked sadly, but she knew that going back to sleep wouldn't help. There was no way that she would be able to recapture the feeling that Ben was really there.

Taking a clean washcloth and towel from the linen closet, she went into the bathroom to wash up. It was then she realized that the graythings had cleared out of her apartment, at least temporarily. Her reflection in the mirror was clear, and the tiles in the shower were not covered with grayish slime. She took a quick shower, relishing the feel of the fresh, clean water on her face and body.

Gray scum ran off her hair, but as she watched, it was sucked into the drain and carried away.

When she emerged from the shower, Mariele felt better than she had for days. The heaviness in her heart hadn't lifted. She was still angry with all the players in the deadly game Ben had gotten her involved in, and she still hadn't made a decision about whether she wanted to live or die, if she had a choice, but she did feel better.

Dressed in jeans and a warm sweater, she took another ride on the elevator. The fifth floor was silent, but it was a strange silence. Mariele had the feeling that she had stepped off the elevator just as the noise stopped and the quiet began. It was as if there were echoes in the silence, ready to explode at any second. The air down here was full of water, and perspiration formed on her forehead as she walked down the hallway. Was this where all the graythings had gone when they left her apartment? She hesitated, but she knew that she had to get inside and talk to Bruce, to give him a chance to tell her whatever it was he had wanted to tell her in the middle of the night.

The door stood slightly ajar, but Bruce didn't come when she rang the doorbell. He didn't come when she pounded, or when she hammered as hard as she could. Why in the world would he go out and leave the door unlocked? she wondered. Then, she laughed aloud, remembering that she had recently done the very same thing, leaving the graythings to deal with anyone who had the nerve to break and enter her apartment.

"All right, Bruce," she said aloud, but not too loudly, "I'm coming in now."

Putting her shoulder against the door, she shoved hard and felt the door move. It had been stuck, that's all. She'd call the super when she got back upstairs and tell him that several of the doors in the building needed to be repaired so that they wouldn't stick every time it was humid.

"Bruce, are you here? If you want to talk to me, this is your last chance."

The rooms literally buzzed with silence. Mariele was learning fast that silence isn't simply the absence of sound. Silence has its own sound, and Bruce's apartment was full to overflowing with it.

"Bruce, don't play games with me. I'm going to leave if you don't show yourself right now."

The kitchen was empty, as were the living room, dining room, and the smaller of the two bedrooms, the one Bruce used as a study. The door to the master bedroom was closed, and Mariele seriously considered walking out of the apartment without opening it.

"Bruce?" She called his name again, her mouth close to the door. Nothing. The door was tightly closed, and if it had been locked, Mariele would have welcomed the chance to retreat. Instead, she turned the knob, and the door moved slowly inward, revealing a room more feminine in its furnishings than she would have expected of Bruce. The walls were sea-foam green, and the curtains matched the bedspread. Both were of a flowered print mixing the same sea-foam hue with several shades of blue. The effect was beautiful and restful, and Mariele was tempted to lie down on the queen-size bed and close her eyes. She shook her head and closed the bedroom door, then turned toward the only door she hadn't opened yet.

Sweat dripped from her forehead and stung her eyes, as she tried to get up the courage to tackle the bathroom.

"Are you in there?" she asked quietly. "Are you in there, Bruce?"

There was a sound, she was sure of it. A low moaning that reminded her of wind sighing through the pines on a cold winter's day in Vermont, where Ben's sister lived. Ben had loved it there, but Mariele hadn't cared for the bitter cold and the awful desolation of being at the mercy of the elements for months each year.

That was exactly how she felt now, at the mercy of elements over which she held no control.

"Is that you, Bruce? Are you sick?" With her hand on the knob, she turned it slowly, then let it roll back to its original position. Sweat on her hands kept her from holding onto it. Try again, she told herself. Bruce may be sick, he may need help.

Hands on the knob. Both hands this time. Turn it slowly, apply pressure when it starts to slip back. Push. Put your weight against it. The door didn't budge. One more time, throw your hip into it, all your weight. It moved a half an inch, then slammed against her and took back what ground she had gained. She leaned against the wall beside the door and panted until her breath came normally again.

One more try, then she'd go for help. She knew Bruce was in there, she felt it. Positioning herself in front of the door, she raised her right leg and kicked, simultaneously placing both hands flat on the door and pushing hard.

It moved a few feet inward, then stopped. Hot, humid air rushed out and hit Mariele in the face. Within seconds, she was covered with the clammy perspiration she now associated with the gray-things, but she was determined to open that last door. She leaned against it, but it felt to her as if it had met with an obstruction that prevented it from opening wider. When several attempts failed to move the obstacle in the door's path, Mariele edged around the door and let herself into the bathroom.

She didn't scream hysterically at the sight of her former friend swinging from the ceiling. Horror and fear filled her mind and body, making it impossible for her to move from the spot, even though she wanted to run from the apartment and summon help. A more practical side of her said that there was nothing that could help Bruce now. His eyes were bloodshot, nearly bulging out of his head. His face was blue, and his mouth was twisted into a grimace of pain and terror.

"Oh, Bruce, I'm sorry." Mariele touched his legs to stop their swinging, which obviously had been started by the impact of the door hitting them. She finally was able to look away from him and put her hands over her eyes to shut out the grizzly scene. It had been set up to look like he had committed suicide, but she knew that wasn't the case.

It was difficult to navigate her way through the apartment. The air was thick and greenish-gray, like pea soup, and the furniture seemed to have been moved around since she entered the apartment minutes before. She kept bumping into things and tripping over things strewn on the floor.

The elevator was slow, and that gave her time to regain control and compose herself. In her apartment, she dialed 911 and reported a murder in Bruce's apartment. Dutifully, she gave her name and apartment number and said she would wait for the police there.

They arrived in fifteen minutes, obviously not in a hurry. I guess, she figured, if the victim already is dead, there's not much they can do to help him, so why hurry. She heard the sirens first, then walked to the window and watched them arrive, two patrol cars and one unmarked car. They took their time entering the building, looking around carefully and checking out the street before leaving it. When she could no longer see them on the street, she opened the door and waited for them to come for her.

What followed was one of the worst events of her life, right up there behind losing Ben and learning that she had given birth to a child. The officer, who was left with her in the apartment, wouldn't let her go back downstairs to show them what she had seen. When a detective, a cynical older man, came up, he told her that they had not found a body hanging in the bathroom.

"Why did you lie to us, Mrs. Hollander?"

Her mind went blank, so she said nothing in reply. "Why didn't you tell us that the body was in the bedroom?"

"It wasn't. It was hanging in the bathroom."

"Hanging from what? There are no hooks of any kind in the bathroom ceiling, and there was no rope around the victim's neck."

Mariele looked up and met the detective's accusing brown eyes. She knew then that they were never going to believe her.

"I don't know what it was hanging from, I just know that it . . . Bruce's body was hanging. Someone hung Bruce, and he was my friend." Tears ran down her cheeks, and sobs shook her body, but the detective had no sympathy for her.

"Mrs. Hollander, I'm going to have to ask you to come down to the station with us."

"Why? Is it a crime to report a murder? Should I have just kept my mouth shut and let someone else call you, even if it was weeks before they found the body?"

"No, you did the right thing by calling us. But we need to find out why you went down there in the first place and why you lied to us about the location of the body and about what you thought to be the cause of death."

"I'm not a doctor, but it seemed pretty obvious that the cause of death was—"

"Excuse me, but the body wasn't hanging when we found it, let's get that straight. The body was in the bedroom, close to the windows. It looked to us as if he had been pounding on the windows, trying to escape someone or something. Or maybe trying to call for help."

"Do you think he killed himself?"

"We haven't made that determination yet. Now, if you'll get your coat, the officer will drive you to the precinct."

And so it had gone for hours, until Mariele was almost dead on her feet from exhaustion. After asking the same questions over and over for what seemed like hundreds of times, they left her alone for a long time. Finally, a younger detective came back into the interrogation room and announced that she was free to go. Of course, they would be getting in touch with her again soon. Meanwhile, she was not to leave the city.

The police offered to drive her home, but she preferred to take a cab. The driver kept staring at her in his rearview mirror and asking if she was all right, until she realized that she had been laughing out loud. "I can't leave the city," she told him confidentially, scaring the hell out of him. "Why don't they try telling that to the graythings?"

eighteen

Mariele gave the cab driver her last ten-dollar bill, which reminded her that she would have to make a trip to the bank and transfer some funds from her savings into her checking account. It was sad to think that Ben had saved so carefully for so long, and that his hard-earned money was now being used to pay for taxicabs and Chinese takeout. It saddened Mariele even further to think of the lovely business she had built up from scratch and how there was barely a client left who even would take her calls.

There was a long, rambling message from Simon on her machine. He went on and on about how she should be grateful to be alive. "You're lucky Dwago didn't just kill you on the spot when you showed up in Fort Lee," he said, but somehow, Mariele didn't feel lucky. Bruce was dead, and she wondered if Dwago and Simon would be able to continue to outsmart the graythings much longer.

She pushed the erase button and waited for the tape to clear itself, then she reached for the phone to call Simon. A hand came out of nowhere and clamped over hers on the telephone receiver. She hated to admit that it scared her even more than the graythings did. Trembling, Mariele turned to look into the face of the intruder.

It was such a shock that for a minute she forgot to remember that the tiny woman who stood beside her had broken into her home and still had a small clawlike hand fastened tightly over hers. If Simon had a sister, this could have been her. She looked enough like Valda Novak to be her daughter—the same frail frame, the same child's face with the dark, piercing eyes. But Valda Novak had to be ancient, maybe over a hundred years old, while this woman appeared to be in her fifties. When Mariele saw her, Valda's skin had been wrinkled and worn; this woman's skin was flawless.

"Who are you?" Mariele asked, coming to grips with the situation. "And what in the hell are you doing in my apartment?"

"Don't you remember me, dear?" the woman asked. Her voice was gratingly familiar, but Mariele couldn't believe what her ears told her. "Such a lovely, sweet girl, Mariele. Such a shame that you ever got in with these awful people."

"People like your son?" Mariele asked, believing the truth at last.

The woman sighed and loosened her grip on Mariele's hand. "Unfortunately, my Simon is almost as blameful as the others. He should have given up years ago and saved us all a great deal of misery, including you, dear."

"I asked you a question," Mariele said, pulling

her hand free and moving away from Valda. "What are you doing here?"

"I have decided to save you from the dark forces that are insinuating themselves into your body and your mind," the woman answered. "When your mind belongs to them, they will take your soul, because you will offer no resistance then."

"The graythings haven't taken my mind away from me yet, and so far I've done a damned good job of fighting them off without your help."

"That is not the truth, my child. If you tell me that you have not contemplated suicide, or had the desire to give up and let them have your body, you will be lying, both to me and to yourself."

"Only in moments of despair," Mariele whispered, and her own words convinced her that what Valda said was true, the graythings were slowly, insidiously taking over her mind.

"You will never be able to forgive me for my part in your tragedy," the older woman continued, "but I must, at least, try to explain to you what is happening."

"Yes," Mariele agreed, "I need to know."

"Would it be too presumptuous of me to ask for a cup of tea to ease my throat while I talk?"

"No, let's go to the kitchen and sit down. The graythings haven't come back yet, but I'm sure they will."

"They will come soon," Valda agreed, shuddering at the thought.

While Mariele heated water and prepared tea, Valda began to talk. Her words flowed rapidly, as if she had to finish her story before the graythings came and stopped the words, or possibly the thoughts behind the words.

"When my son was a very young man," she said, "he fell in love with a woman who didn't return his affection. In the way of so many of the young who suffer unrequited love, he decided that life was not worth living without her. He walked into the ocean, planning to drown himself."

Mariele gasped and instinctively reached out for Valda's hand. It was difficult to imagine the suave, self-confident Simon trying to take his own life over a girl who didn't love him.

"Go on," Mariele urged, when Valda had composed herself.

"Simon didn't die, but his heart stopped beating for several minutes before he was revived by an overzealous swimmer who pulled him out of the water. My son came very close to dying. He was in a coma for several days, and his recuperation took months. During that time, he told me about the graythings. They had come to him during his time in the coma and told him that his soul belonged to them."

When Mariele looked puzzled, Valda tried to explain. "When you make the decision to commit suicide, you make a sometimes unconscious decision to give your body to the graythings. Satan has given them the power to take the bodies and the souls of suicides or their surrogates.

"This is what they told Simon when he was in the coma. He had gone too far to back out and change his mind, so they had come to claim his body. Since he had changed his mind by then and decided that he wanted to live, the graythings demanded another body to replace the one they had expected to receive that day.

"Simon was frantic. He had realized that the woman he was involved with wasn't worth his life, so he pleaded with the graythings to spare him."

Valda paused to catch her breath, and Mariele poured more tea while she waited for the woman to continue.

"Selfishly, he tried to offer them the body of the young woman who had until recently been the object of his affections and the cause of his predicament. But they told him that her body was not his to offer. The substitute had to be either a spouse, a blood relative, or a newborn child."

"Did they tell him why?" Mariele asked. "It would seem that if they wanted a body or a soul badly enough, they wouldn't be so particular."

"Those are the rules, that's all I know," Valda answered shortly, "and Simon had to abide by them. His sister and I were his only living blood relatives, and of course, he was not married and never had been. He wouldn't give up either his mother or his sister, and he told them so. He fought them valiantly, although they made his life miserable for several weeks.

"I'm not sure to this day what happened next. Maybe they wore him down, or maybe they got tired of waiting and broke through the boundaries that had been set for them. Anyway, they took his sister.

We heard her screaming from downstairs, but when we tried to go to her, the steps had disappeared. When the police finally came, the steps were back where they belonged, but Joyce was dead. Her body had been cut to shreds by some kind of razor-sharp instrument. There was an autopsy and an investigation, but her killer never was found. Of course, for a long time, Simon and I were suspects. We didn't find out until the autopsy results came down that she was four months pregnant."

"Oh, my God!"

"It almost killed Simon. He never has been the same since, either mentally or physically. The graythings damaged his body and his soul that day."

"But I still don't understand what claim they have on you. Have they been hounding you all these years because your son cheated them, even though you had nothing to do with that?"

"They wanted me to take his place when Simon backed out on going with them. When I refused, that seems to have given them the power to come after me."

There was silence in the kitchen for the next few minutes, as both women sipped their tepid tea and thought about what Valda had said. It was Mariele who spoke first.

"Where are they now?" she asked. "Why aren't they here?"

Valda laughed bitterly before she answered, "Oh, they are here, my child. You must learn that only sometimes they drip and run and stink. Other times, they watch and wait from their own dimension, where we cannot see them. For each one you see, there are thousands of them hovering nearby, fighting for their chance to get into your world and your life. If you knew how many of them are out there, waiting, just out of reach, you would go mad with fear."

"If you've seen them, how have you survived without losing your mind?" Mariele asked, thinking that Valda might be stretching the truth.

"Do you think I have?" the woman answered. "I have barely survived over the years, and then only with the help of others like me. And how do you know that I have kept my sanity intact?"

"You look much younger than you did when I saw you in the hospital," Mariele blurted out. She hoped that the element of surprise might prevent Valda from making up a good excuse for the change in her appearance.

"I was there for my treatment," the older woman answered. "I used the time to contact you, so that Simon could meet you."

"Why? Why did Simon want to meet me?"

"He learned about you from Ben before Ben passed over, and he felt compassion for what he thought you must be going through. He thought that he might be a comfort to you."

"But why such an elaborate ruse? Why didn't he just knock on the door and tell me that he was a friend of Ben's?"

"That isn't Simon's way."

"He knew about the baby?"

"Yes, he knew. He wanted to comfort you."

"You still haven't told me why you look so much younger now," Mariele asked insistently.

"I told you, my dear. I was there for my treatment. I have them every few months, and this is how I look for a short time afterward. It won't be long now, and I'll have to go again. That's why I'm here, to offer you my help before I go away again."

"I don't know how you think you can help me, unless you want to tell me how you helped them take my baby." Mariele didn't know by what miracle she was able to have this conversation without screaming with pain, but somehow, she was staying calm enough to talk things out.

Valda didn't answer immediately, and Mariele noticed that she was blotting her forehead with a napkin. Her other hand was busy loosening the collar of her black dress.

"Are you all right?"

The woman tried to shake her head, but she was trembling so violently that her head bobbed back and forth on her neck, then fell toward her chest as she lost consciousness.

Mariele was torn between letting the woman die for her part in stealing Allison and a lifelong respect for human life, whether it was deserved or not. What finally spurred her to action was the realization that if Valda died, that would be two deaths in the same building within twenty-four hours of each other. And two deaths in which Mariele Hollander somehow was involved. If the police were puzzled about Bruce's death, Valda's would point them directly to Mariele.

She ran around the table and lifted Valda's head. The woman's eyes had rolled up into her head, and her skin was gray and clammy. Her pulse was dangerously slow. Mariele lifted the frail woman in her arms and carried her to the bedroom, where she placed her gently in the middle of the bed. Then, she went to the bathroom and made a cold compress from a hand towel. While she applied the cold compress to Valda's forehead and then to her neck, Mariele spoke to her, saying her name over and over, until she finally stirred.

When Valda opened her eyes, they were filled with fear.

"Where am I?" she asked, glancing fearfully around the unfamiliar room.

"You're in my bedroom. We were in the kitchen when you suddenly became ill and lost consciousness. I carried you in here."

Valda squeezed Mariele's hand and looked deep into her eyes before she spoke.

"You're a good woman, Mariele. No one would have blamed you if you had let me go."

"The police would have blamed me," Mariele answered, and then, incongruously, she and Valda both began to laugh. After less than a minute, the older woman was gasping for breath. As Mariele stood several feet away and observed Valda's struggles, she wondered about her true age. Right this moment, she no longer appeared to be close to

Simon's age. She was wrinkled and gray, and she could have been ancient.

When Valda was breathing easier again, she stretched out her arms and motioned for Mariele to come to her side. Mariele sat down on the side of the bed, and Valda clamped both of her hands on Mariele's arms. Mariele felt her skin growing hot and moist where the woman's hands were touching her, but struggling only strengthened the contact between them.

"Go to Simon," the old woman whispered. "Go to Simon now. He needs you, Mariele. My son needs you. Go to him now."

Her words and the tone of her voice were hypnotic. When she released her grip on Mariele's arms, Mariele found herself going to the closet for her coat. "Simon needs me," she repeated to herself as she waited for the elevator. Without realizing what she was doing, she lifted the sleeve of her coat and rubbed at the skin of her right arm, which the older woman's touch had left wet and puckered. If she had looked at it, she would have seen that the crimped skin had a greenish-gray cast.

"I must go to Simon," Mariele said as the elevator doors opened to admit her. "I must go to Simon."

nineteen

Mariele stood in the open doorway and watched him for several minutes before she let him know that she was there. Simon looked as if he just had stepped off the pages of an F. Scott Fitzgerald novel. As he paced back and forth across his small living room, his red paisley robe rippled around his trim body. His expressive hands worried his longish silver hair that framed a nearly perfect face. Mariele could see why Valda loved her son so dearly.

"I love him, too," she whispered too softly for him to hear. Still, he turned and saw her there, and she caught the relief in his eyes before the daggers started flying.

"Mariele! Where have you been? Why in the hell haven't you returned my calls? I've pounded on your door, I've left messages on your machine."

He crossed the room, dragged her inside, and slammed and bolted the door behind her, all in what seemed like one graceful movement. His head rested on her shoulder, and for a moment, she didn't realize that he was crying.

"I thought you were dead," he sobbed. "As God

is my witness, I thought the crazy bastard had killed you."

She put both hands on his head and ran her fingers through his soft hair, while she guided his face to her chest.

"It's all right, Simon," she whispered. "I'm here now, and everything will be all right."

He nuzzled against her for a long time before he finally lifted his head to look at her. He really had been crying. His pale blue eyes were red, and the remnants of tears clung to his eyelids.

"This is some role reversal," he said, trying to smile. "I'm supposed to be the one comforting you." Then, he said, too seriously, "Oh, Mariele, you don't have any idea how much I care for you."

She brought her mouth to his and kissed him hard, the way she always had wanted to, and eventually, he kissed her back. When he started to push her away, she clung to him and refused to let go.

"Please, Simon, I need you, don't push me away."

"I don't want to," he moaned. "God knows I don't want to."

"There's no reason why it can't happen," Mariele reasoned. "We're both free, and it's been over a year since Ben died. I can't go on mourning forever."

"It isn't that. Please, Mariele, we have to talk." He grabbed both of her arms and held them rigid at her sides. "There are so many things you don't know."

"I know more than you think," she answered,

leaning toward him, planting tiny kisses on his cheeks and on the edges of his lips.

"Stop it, Mariele," he demanded, shaking her to get her attention.

"All right, we'll talk," she agreed, not giving up, "but I want you, Simon, and I intend to have you. You're just postponing the inevitable."

She expected a smile from him, at the least, but his eyes were sad and deadly serious.

"My mother has talked to you," he stated, once Mariele was seated on the couch, and he was sitting in an easy chair directly across from her.

She didn't ask how he knew; there was a telephone on the bedstand within reach of where she had left Valda lying on the bed.

"She told me everything, Simon, and none of it matters now."

"She only told you what she knows. There is something else you have to hear."

"I'm tired of hearing it! The graythings have Ben, they want you and Valda, they're coming for me. I don't care anymore. I only care about wanting someone to love me and comfort me until they come. That's all I want now, Simon."

She could tell that he desired to come to her, but he did an admirable job of restraining himself. He clung to the arms of his chair and kept his feet planted firmly on the floor. Only the pain in his eyes gave him away.

"My sister was only twenty-four when she died," he said, after a few more minutes. "She was four months pregnant. She was in love and planning to

be married. I cheated her out of her chance for
happiness. How can you respect me after knowing
what I did?"

"It wasn't your fault," Mariele said, starting to
rise from the couch. He waved her back, disagree-
ing with her assessment of his guilt.

"Valda told me how it happened. If she doesn't
blame you for what happened, what makes you
think that I won't forgive you?"

"I killed her," he said.

"What?" Mariele asked, hoping that she had
heard wrong.

"I gave them my sister to save my own skin. I
should have given them my mother, but I couldn't
bear to do that. So, I gave them my sister and her
unborn child."

"Even . . . even if this is true," Mariele said,
stumbling over her words, "you didn't know about
her pregnancy. Surely, if you had known—"

"I knew."

"Simon, please, you're confusing me."

"It's all very simple, Mariele. There's really nothing to be confused about. I had decided that I
wanted to live, and I had two choices, give them my
mother or give them my sister. If I did that, they
swore they would let me alone, let me go on to live
a normal life. That was supposed to put an end to
my obligation. Can you believe that I was stupid
enough to think they would tell me the truth?"

Mariele was looking at him, but she found it
difficult to see his face. His features were blurred
and fuzzy, as if she was seeing him through a veil.

"Don't cry, Mariele, I'm not worth your tears."

"I'm not crying for you," she said angrily. "I'm crying for your sister and her child, and for my child."

"It wouldn't do any good for me to say how sorry I am."

"No, it wouldn't."

"If I had just been able to drown myself," Simon said wistfully, "that would have been the end of it for me. My sister would be alive, and my mother could have lived out her normal life span in peace."

Mariele took advantage of Simon's preoccupation with his own failings to find out about Valda's involvement. "How did they get their hands on your mother?" she asked. "I thought they could only come after you if someone offered you to them."

"Not true," Simon said, obviously eager to explain. "Ben didn't offer you. He wouldn't. The whole idea of conceiving a child was used to save you from the graythings. And, then, it was erased from your memory so that you wouldn't feel the pain of loss. It was effective until your dream and finding Ben's diary brought it all back to you."

"How do you fit into all this, Simon? I mean, you and Ben. You'd be an unlikely choice for Ben's friendship and vice versa. You're nothing alike and probably had very little in common."

"I'm surprised that you didn't figure it out on your own by now. I was the one who erased the pregnancy and the birth from your memory. Then, I filled your mind with other things so that the

months you spent married to Ben wouldn't be so
glaringly empty."

"Are you saying that my memories of my married life were manufactured?"

"Not necessarily."

"How will I ever know again which memories
are real and which ones were pulled out of thin
air to fill up the blank spaces in my life?"

"I'm here for you now, Mariele. I can help you."

"No offense, Simon," she cut in, "but when I
feel like reminiscing about Ben, I don't think I
want you there interpreting my memories for me."

Simon raised his hands in a hopeless gesture
that made Mariele want to go to him and wrap
her arms around him.

"I didn't mean that, Simon," she said. "It's just
that I feel so helpless. My husband is gone, and
my baby is dead, and now, I find out that you're
not the person I thought you were. Sometimes, I
amaze myself with my self-control. If I went crazy
and tried to kill all of you, I don't think any jury
would convict me."

"I don't blame you for hating me," Simon answered. "I deserve your hatred."

"I don't hate you, Simon." Mariele rose from
the couch and crossed the room to kneel before
Simon's chair. "You've been such a comfort to me
these past months. I couldn't have faced them
without you."

She pressed close to Simon and laid her cheek
against his. Her left hand moved upward so that
her fingers could touch his lips and caress his face.

Relaxing, she let her body fall to the left. The move surprised Simon and put him off guard. It was easy for her to reach out with her right hand and open the paisley robe that was belted tightly around his waist. Then, she used both hands to rip open the white shirt he wore beneath the robe.

She looked down at Simon's chest, even as he pushed at her body and tried to get out of the chair where he was trapped. What she saw there brought bile from her roiling stomach up her throat and into her mouth. She put her hand up to hold back the nausea that threatened her and tried to look away. It was Simon's hands that held her head in a steady position. She could close her eyes, but she couldn't turn away to escape the awful sight in front of her.

Simon's chest was rotten, that was the only way to describe it. The skin, if you even could call it skin, was a horrible gray color, covered with festering green sores. In some places, it was so thin that you could see through to the organs beneath. Everything in Simon's chest was decaying; even his bones were tinged with sickly green. As Mariele watched in shock, he pulled at his undershorts, to reveal his stomach and his genitalia. His penis was shrunken and shriveled, and a tiny green worm rested on his concave stomach.

"Now, you know why I couldn't make love to you," he spat out, splattering her face with spittle. "I can't make love because I'm not a man, although I still have the mind of a man, and my poor dying heart still beats like a man's heart."

When he had finished speaking, Simon looked away, as if he were truly ashamed that anyone had seen him that way. As if his body was the direct result of his actions. When Mariele tried to get away from him, he didn't resist her. He loosened his grip on her head and dropped his arms to his sides. She lifted herself out of the chair, being careful not to touch Simon's body. Her care was due to the fact that the sight of his open wounds disgusted her, but also because he looked so fragile, as if any small amount of pressure might tear his paper-thin skin and rupture his diseased internal organs.

A frantic search for her coat didn't turn it up, and she was ready to leave without it when Simon spoke to her again and stopped her in her tracks.

"Mariele, if we had met years ago, you would have married me and saved me from this."

"No."

"Yes. And all I ask of you now is words. I didn't lie to you. I told you that we couldn't make love. If you had just listened."

"I need to get some air."

"It's too cold outside. Open the window in the kitchen and sit in there while you make your decision."

"My decision?"

"As to whether or not you'll stand by me, now that you know the truth about what I really am."

"Why should I?" she asked, turning away from him.

But Mariele did as he suggested, and the crisp,

arctic air cleared her head fast. When she returned to the living room, Simon hadn't moved from the chair. He hadn't even bothered to adjust his clothing to cover his nakedness but he did so now.

"Is this what's wrong with Valda, too? Is that why she has to go to the hospital for treatments?"

Simon nodded and looked into Mariele's eyes. "You know what this means, don't you?"

"I think so. I don't understand it, but I think it means that you're turning into one of them, even though you're still alive."

"You're a very intelligent woman and a very honest one. You could make this much more difficult for me, if you chose to do so. The truth is that with every day that passes I become less of a man and more of a graything. A graything, *thing* being the operative word here."

"I don't know what to say."

"There's nothing you can say. Ben was smart to take the easy way out, before this started happening to him, too."

"But if you gave them another soul . . . I'm afraid I just don't understand any of this."

Simon laughed harshly, and the sound penetrated straight to Mariele's soul. "The graythings are the devil's own, Mariele. They are creatures who dwell in the depths of hell. Why should we expect them to be fair?"

twenty

Seated in the back of the taxicab with Simon, Mariele was decidedly uncomfortable. She couldn't help but remember what was beneath his shirt and the fashionable leather jacket that he now wore. If she was thrown against him by the driver's eratic maneuvers, she was sure she would scream. Thankfully, Simon seemed to be fully aware of the way she felt about him now that she knew his deepest, darkest secrets.

He had decided, after hours of introspection, that he must confess to Valda that he had sacrificed his sister and her unborn child to save his own life. Mariele still was trying to convince him otherwise.

"I wish you'd think this through a little more thoroughly, Simon," she urged, as the cab sped uptown, closer to her apartment.

"I will never have a moment's peace until she knows the truth, Mariele," he said, with a dramatic flourish of his expressive hands.

"Do you think this will bring her peace? She loves you so desperately, you're all she has."

"Do you believe in life after death?" he asked, veering off the subject.

"What has that got to do with your telling Valda?"

"Just answer the question, please."

"I don't know anymore. When Ben and I first met, he believed in reincarnation. After reading some of his books and listening to several of his lectures, I believed, too. I truly believed that this lifetime was merely a steppingstone on the path to perfection."

"And that's rather difficult to believe now that you know about the graythings, right?"

Mariele started to laugh, but she quickly gained control of herself. "Simon, you are a master of understatement."

"If there is another life, either with the graythings or back on this earth, Valda eventually will learn what I've done, from me or from some other source. If she has to know, she must hear it from me."

Mariele nodded, knowing that it was useless to argue with him. Still, as the cab drew up in front of her building, she felt like telling the driver to pull away and leave Simon on the sidewalk. She dreaded the next few minutes and the pain that Simon intended to inflict on his mother. Maybe, she should just come out and tell him that she regarded his decision as another act of selfishness.

"You don't have to come up with me," he said, as the cab pulled away from the curb and merged with the late-day traffic.

She shrugged and entered the lobby with her head down, so that she wouldn't have to exchange pleasantries with any of the doormen. The upcoming confrontation with Valda was obviously bothering her a lot more than it was bothering Simon.

"Don't worry so much," he said, and she wondered if he really could read her mind. "My mother is a very strong woman."

"All right." He reached for her hand and squeezed it, sending small waves of revulsion up and down her body. The thought that just hours ago she had wanted to go to bed with him probably would have made her vomit if she'd any food in her stomach.

The minute the elevator stopped on her floor, Mariele sensed that something was wrong. It was nothing concrete, just a feeling, but she was learning to go with her feelings. More often than not, they were proving to be right on target.

Simon obviously felt something, too. He beat Mariele off the elevator and practically ran down the hallway to her apartment door. From several feet away, she saw him turn the doorknob and open the door without the key, which she was clutching in her hand. He moved through the door, then stopped so abruptly that she ran into him in the entryway.

"Simon, what is it? Oh, my God!"

The apartment had been completely trashed. At first glance, it seemed as if nothing was left intact. The living room was a shambles of torn pillows, broken glass, and beloved books ripped to shreds and thrown into a huge pile in the middle of the floor. Stuffing oozed from the arms and seat of Mariele's beautiful couch, and her carefully chosen fruitwood tables were covered with gouges and scratches. Even the carpeting had been mutilated.

"Somebody really did a job on this place," Simon remarked, but Mariele couldn't find the words to answer.

They stood there for a long time before a low, guttural sound issued from Simon's throat. Mariele barely recognized the word as "Mother." He suddenly was propelled toward the bedroom with Mariele close on his heels. She was more frightened than she had been in a long time, because she didn't know her enemy.

"Who did this, Simon?" she asked, but he probably didn't hear her. At least, he didn't answer. He entered the bedroom and made his way to the bed where his mother lay, not bothering to step around what was left of Mariele's clothes and jewelry. This room was worse than the living room, probably because they'd had more to work with—cosmetics and perfumes, designer suits and dresses, and cherished heirlooms that had belonged to Mariele's grandmother.

Only the bed was intact, and in the middle of the bed lay Simon's dead mother. They hadn't bothered to close her eyes, or to wipe the spittle from her mouth. Her last moments must have been the most frightening of her life, and whoever had killed her wanted Simon to know that. There were red blotches on her face, and her arms rested at odd angles to her body, as if they had been snapped like matchsticks.

But the worst thing, the thing that Mariele knew had been done for her benefit, was Valda's nakedness. Her torso was that of an old woman, overweight and wrinkled, an unattractive sight even if she had been an ordinary woman. But Valda was not ordinary. She was a human being who had sold out to the graythings—or maybe she had been sold out by her son. Her legs and arms looked almost normal, as if the worst sight, the greatest shock had been kept under wraps until the moment of her death, so that Valda could continue to live among the other members of the human race.

The trunk of her body was a replica of Simon's chest and stomach, only worse. Much worse. Mariele thought she saw something move on Valda's chest, and she moved a few steps closer to the bed. There was something moving—worms. Tiny, wet gray worms were crawling in and out of holes in Valda's withered breasts.

Mariele turned away and gagged, but nothing came up. She couldn't even remember when she had eaten last, and she was glad that was the case. It sickened her to think that she and Valda had spent time together in the kitchen and that she had stood so close to the woman and held her hands. Now, Valda was lying in Mariele's bed, dead, with gray worms finishing up the job of devouring her internal organs.

"Simon, please," Mariele begged, when he gave no sign of leaving his mother's side. The top of his body was literally draped over Valda's, and Mariele imagined that the worms were slithering onto his skin, anticipating the time when they could invade his chest as they had Valda's. When Simon finally stood and moved away from the bed, Mariele's nostrils were filled with the stench of rotting flesh. Again, she was glad that she had only the memory of food to keep down.

"Who did this?" When they were back in the living room, Mariele repeated the question she had asked earlier.

"The graythings did it, Mariele," he answered angrily. "I thought you knew that. The graythings killed my mother because she wouldn't accept the terrible ideas they put in her head and because they were tired of waiting for her to die a natural death."

"But all this physical damage. Why would they trash my apartment this way and ruin so many material things?"

"That's very simple. They want you to despair and go with them willingly." Simon stood in the middle of the living-room floor with his hands on his hips, surveying the wreckage of Mariele's life. "What do you want to salvage? If we can do it quickly, I'll stay and help you sort it out."

"No," Mariele answered, letting her eyes see only what Simon's saw, "I don't want any of it."

"You don't want it? Photographs of Ben, things that he gave you, memories?"

"I have my memories, but I'm not sure they're worth saving either. Come on, let's get out of here."

Mariele walked briskly out of the apartment and

down the hallway to the elevator without looking back. She probably would have cried if she was alone, but she wouldn't let Simon see her with her defenses down. She wasn't sure which side he was on now, hers or theirs.

"Where will you go?" he asked on the sidewalk, as if maybe he meant to part company with her there.

"Right now? I don't know."

"You don't want to go with me, trust me on that."

"Where are you going?"

"I'm going to give them as much hell as I can possibly muster. I'm going to make a lot of noise about what they did to my mother. Does that sound stupid? It is, but that isn't going to stop me."

"I just realized that they aren't in my apartment now," Mariele said, as she followed Simon to the curb, where he was trying to flag down a taxi. "You're acting as if you know where they are."

"I do know where they are. Do you want me to introduce you?"

"I wish you'd quit making jokes. This isn't a game, Simon."

"Oh, yes, it is." He laughed bitterly and opened the back door of a battered vehicle that was posing as a taxi. "Everything's a game, Mariele. Everyone knows that life's a game, so what makes you think that death isn't also a game?"

Simon climbed into the cab and gave the driver

an address. He started to close the door, then stopped to give her one last chance.

"Are you coming or not?" he asked. Mariele took the hand that he offered, and he pulled her into the dark interior of the cab just as the driver put it into gear and took off.

"You're not a very good detective," he said moments later. The cab was stuck in Manhattan gridlock, and Simon was letting his impatience show. "I would have thought you'd have it figured out by now."

"I told you, I didn't know it was a game, and I'm not a very good investigator anyway."

He gave her a look that said he was more than a little disappointed with her. He also seemed to be contemplating how to tell her what he wanted her to know.

"Did you ever wonder why Ben was taken to Manhattan Hospital after his accident?" he asked finally.

"I guess I assumed that maybe their emergency room was empty. To tell you the truth, I never asked, so I really don't know."

"Manhattan Hospital is a small, private hospital, privately funded. It's little more than a well-equipped clinic actually. The general public is seldom admitted to Manhattan Hospital."

"That's very interesting, but if all the other emergency rooms were busy that night, it's possible that the EMS would have taken him there, isn't it?"

"Did you imagine that it was a coincidence that

Valda called you to come to the same hospital when she contacted you?"

"I thought it was a coincidence, yes."

"And you also thought it was a coincidence that Dwago is employed there?"

"What?" Mariele's outburst brought a long, searching glance in the rearview mirror from their stoic cabbie.

"Why didn't you tell me?" she demanded of Simon in a more subdued tone of voice.

"You told me you were having him checked out."

"I haven't had time. Now, I certainly wish I had. Please, don't tell me that maniac is a doctor."

"He's on the staff. I don't know exactly what his job title is, but I know he didn't attend medical school, so there's little chance of their handing him a scalpel and letting him perform brain surgery."

"Did he kill Ben?" She didn't think that was possible, but it was a question she felt compelled to ask.

"Everything you've been told about Ben's death is the truth. Dwago had little, if anything, to do with it."

"I'm not trying to find a way to shift blame."

"No one accused you of that."

The cab moved forward and broke free from the gridlocked traffic. They rode in silence for several minutes before Mariele spoke again.

"Are we going there now to confront the gray . . ." She looked up, met the cabbie's eyes in the mirror,

and changed her mind about filling his ears with
things he really didn't need to know. ". . . to confront them?" she finished.

"Are you frightened?" Simon seemed to care
less what their driver heard or thought of their
conversation.

"Yes."

"I won't force you to go in with me."

"You know I'll go. I have nothing to go home
to anymore."

"You might be risking your life."

"What life?" They smiled at each other, and Simon took her hand. This time, she didn't flinch,
and she actually felt some of the old affection for
him resurface.

twenty-one

This time Mariele was on the lookout for the unusual, and she found it. When she had been to Manhattan Hospital before, she had been in a state of shock, twice traumatized by a midnight phone call. This time, she was alert and paying close attention to her surroundings.

The thing that struck her immediately was that the hospital was too quiet. There was no whisper of nurses' voices, no muted shuffle of their soft-soled shoes on the polished floors. Even the cries of a sick or dying patient were absent from this hospital. True, the first floor could have been well-insulated to keep the normal hospital noises from filtering down to the reception area, but that wasn't the case. Mariele now remembered her last visits, and the awful, unnatural silence that prevailed here. The atmosphere inside these walls was one of a place where the dead were stronger than the living. The dead ruled Manhattan Hospital, and the living hid from the dead behind the closed doors of its sterile rooms.

Mariele and Simon stood in the empty lobby just inside the sliding glass doors that had allowed them entrance. The elderly volunteers who had sat at the reception desk on Mariele's other visits to the hospital were nowhere in sight. If there were such persons on duty, they had abandoned their posts and vanished into the bowels of the white brick building.

Stranger still, there were no visitors or relatives of the sick in sight, and no unintelligible voices booming over the loudspeaker, calling for Dr. Whoever to come to the ER *stat*.

Mariele wondered how she could have ignored all these signs that something was wrong the times she had been here. Well, she hadn't really ignored them. She had simply tucked them away in a corner of her mind because they didn't matter then. Now, she was dredging up things that she hadn't even realized she had noticed at the time.

"Where is everyone?" she asked Simon, who was acting as if he was waiting for a signal of some kind before making his grand entrance.

He shrugged and started walking across the lobby. Mariele had no choice but to follow him, if she didn't want to be left alone in the eerie, abandoned lobby.

"Everyone on staff here has been carefully screened," he explained, stopping halfway across the room. "They all have an interest in what we're doing, either personally or professionally."

"Just what are you doing here, Simon?"

"We're trying to survive, which is something you may want to start thinking about."

Simon was on the move again, before Mariele had a chance to respond to his last remark. He ignored the bank of elevators and opened a door that led down a hallway to a steep flight of stairs. Mariele followed close behind him. At the bottom of the stairs, he put his weight into opening a heavy fire door, and they were in the basement.

It was not nearly as well-lit as the first floor had been. Dim bulbs were recessed in the ceiling, for an atmosphere of gloom and semidarkness in the long corridor that ran from one end of the building to the other.

Simon strode purposefully ahead, until he reached a door several hundred feet from the stairs they had descended. There was a small sign on the door that identified it as the morgue.

Mariele started to back away, but Simon clutched her arm and held her fast.

"No," she told him, "I don't want to go in there. Will you please stop acting so strange? You're starting to scare me, Simon."

"I thought you wanted to see the graythings. Wasn't it you who said you didn't have a life to give up?"

"Well, I've changed my mind. Now, let go of my arm."

She wriggled and tried to get away from him, but Simon's grip on her arm was firm, and he had no intention of letting her get away from him.

He leaned against the door, and it swung inward, releasing an unfamiliar chemical odor into the corridor. Mariele stopped struggling and put her free hand over her nose and mouth to quell the assault of the strong smell that rushed out of the room.

Simon laughed and pushed her into the room

ahead of him. "That's just a strong disinfectant, nothing very sinister at all."

"I'm going to be sick."

"If you were going to lose your lunch, you would have done so a long time ago," he answered matter-of-factly. "Don't worry, you'll get used to the smell in a minute or so."

She didn't get used to it, but she did forget about it, when she realized that there were other things in the room to command her attention. What appeared to be a human form draped with a stained white sheet lay on a metal table in the middle of the long, narrow room. There were two rather large, dirty feet protruding from one end of the sheet, and a small tag dangled from the right big toe.

"Just like in the movies," Mariele whispered, and she laughed hysterically until Simon shook her roughly.

He let go of her arm long enough to hit a switch that filled the room with the powerful overhead light apparently needed for autopsies.

"Why do we need that much light?" Mariele asked, fearful of his answer.

"It will keep the graythings at bay until I'm ready for them," Simon answered, with a twisted smile. "Haven't you noticed that they prefer the dark of night or the gloom of an overcast day to make their appearance?"

"Let's get out of here and go home, Simon," Mariele said softly. "This place is giving me the creeps."

"You have no home left, remember?"

"We could go to your place. I'll fix something to eat. We could stop at the market on our way." Judging from the expression on Simon's face, her try for a touch of normalcy wasn't working. She had no idea what Simon was up to, but she was becoming more frightened by the minute.

"Save your energy, Mariele, I'm not going anyplace, and neither are you.

"Don't try to run," he cautioned, then he moved away from her, still watching her out of the corner of his eye. In the center of the room, he stopped beside the table that had captured Mariele's attention the second they had entered the room.

"Do you know what this is?" he asked.

"Simon, please."

"Do you know what this is?" he repeated louder, using a firm tone of voice.

"I assume that it's a dead body," Mariele answered, angry over the way he was treating her.

"Correct. Absolutely, correct."

With one quick movement, Simon whipped off the sheet to reveal the corpse of a young white male with a jagged wound in his upper chest. The boy was wearing only one article of clothing, a ragged pair of blue jean shorts. Mariele thought he looked pitiful and vulnerable in death.

"Do you know what this man is going to do for me, Mariele?" Simon asked playfully.

"I have no idea."

"Don't turn your eyes away. I want you to look at him, Mariele, because he is going to become a part of me. Such a handsome young lad, isn't he? Such a pity that he had to die so young, don't you agree, Mariele?"

"Yes," she mumbled. "Yes, I agree."

Simon stared at the young man's face, then reached out to stroke it tenderly. Mariele whimpered, and she knew that she was going to lose it. Unless she could convince Simon to start acting rationally, she wasn't going to be able to control her own emotions.

"I'm not going to eat him, Mariele. Is that what you thought I was going to do?"

"I don't know."

"Do you see this lovely young skin?" Simon laid his hand below the wound on the dead man's chest and stroked the skin gently. "This will soon be mine, due to one of the finest plastic surgeons in the state of New York. The procedure is called a skin graft, and it's the miracle of modern medicine that keeps my innards from falling out onto the city streets. Maybe you'd like to watch and see how it's done? I'm sure that could be arranged. But first, we're waiting for a friend of ours to show up and join our little group."

"Simon, I'm watching you change before my eyes, and I don't like what you're changing into. Please, let's go somewhere where we can talk. Please."

Simon had been smiling at her, but a slight noise in the corridor caused him to change his demeanor abruptly. He dragged her over to the far wall and pushed her behind a cabinet, so that the two of them couldn't be seen by anyone entering the room. With his hand clamped over her mouth, he placed his lips close to her ear.

"Shhh," he whispered, "I think one of our guests is arriving a little ahead of schedule."

It was only seconds later that the door eased open and Dwago walked into the brightly lit morgue.

"I know you're in here, Simon," he said loudly. "Did you think your entrance would go unannounced?"

"You are so terribly predictable, Dwago," Simon retorted, taking a step forward. "I set a trap, and you waltzed into it."

Simon pushed Mariele out from behind the cabinet and moved out beside her.

"You know my good friend, Mariele," Simon said to Dwago. "Say hello to our guest, Mariele." When Mariele didn't speak immediately, Simon struck her across the face with his open hand, never taking his eyes off Dwago. She was so surprised by the violence of the attack that she almost passed up her next opportunity to please Simon.

"Hello, Dwago," she said weakly, saving herself from a second blow at the last second.

"How did you get her to come here with you, Simon?" Dwago asked. "How many lies did you have to tell her?"

"Mariele came with me of her own free will, didn't you, Mariele?" Simon asked, as he exerted painful pressure on her shoulder.

She nodded quickly, before he lost his temper again.

"I don't believe that for a moment. You haven't told her what you plan to do with her, have you?"

"Mind your own business, you rotten bastard," Simon screamed. "You only want me to let her go so that you can use her yourself."

"If I wanted her for myself, I would have kept her when I had her in Fort Lee. Why can't you be a man for the first time in your miserable life and tell her what you're going to use her for."

Simon's rage was so unexpected that Mariele cringed away from him in fear: "You used this woman, you raped her in her own bed. Did you ask her permission before you did that?"

"It wasn't necessary to ask, was it, Mariele? By the way, did I ever tell you how good you were? No wonder your husband hated to leave you."

"I said shut up, you bastard!" Simon shoved Mariele out of his way and stood before Dwago in a fighting stance. He extended one hand out in front of him and motioned for Dwago to come to him. If her life hadn't been at stake, Mariele might have thought it was humorous. But all things considered, she thought it was silly and pitiful. She wanted to beg Simon to stop before he got hurt, but given his mood, she was afraid to say anything.

Dwago clearly wasn't afraid of Simon, and Mariele was beginning to think maybe she stood a better chance of surviving if he won the fight that Simon was instigating. He stood at ease, slowly rolling up the sleeves of his black shirt.

"Shouldn't we step outside, Simon?" he asked. "We can settle this out in the parking lot. You can release Mariele and let her go home, then you and I can have a go at it."

"Mariele stays. And we can settle everything right here in this room."

"Really, Simon—" That was as far as Dwago got before Simon leapt across the room and made a lunging motion at Dwago's chest with his right hand. Dwago stepped back quickly, but the room was narrow, and he had little space in which to maneuver. The two men held onto each other and pummeled each other with their fists. Mariele thought of running, but they were wrestling so close to the door that she knew either one of them could grab her if she started for it.

"What you intend to do is wrong, Simon," Dwago said breathlessly. "It's an immoral and unethical act, even for you."

"That's my business," Simon answered. "In case you haven't noticed what's happening here, you won't be around to argue about it."

While Mariele was still trying to figure out what Simon meant by his ominous words, Dwago's head fell forward onto Simon's shoulder. Then, his entire body slumped and slid soundlessly to the floor. He fell at Simon's feet, and Simon used his foot to roll Dwago over onto his back. It was then that Mariele saw the wound in his chest, a deep, perfect cut at least six inches long. She also saw the scalpel that Simon still held in his bloody hand. Then, as she watched, Simon used his heel to crush the side of Dwago's face.

Mariele cried out, but Simon didn't seem to hear her.

twenty-two

While Simon was preoccupied with the further mutilation of Dwago's body, Mariele made a break for the door. Assuming that it swung both ways, she threw herself against it full force. She went barreling out into the hallway, caught her balance, and started running toward the stairs she and Simon had descended earlier, in what seemed like another lifetime.

Simon was right behind her. She could hear his labored breathing and smell the rot that leaked from his chest. She felt his hand touch her jacket, then slide off again, and she knew that it was only a matter of seconds before he overtook her. She turned, moved quickly to the side, and lashed out at him. Lacking the power to kick him in the chest, she planted a powerful blow to the lower part of his stomach.

His screams cut through the silent hospital, and Mariele thought they probably could be heard on every floor. She hoped that someone would hear them and come to her rescue, but she doubted that anyone in the hospital would find screaming unusual.

While Simon was doubled over nursing his injured private parts, Mariele made a run for the elevator. When she got there, the doors were closed. She pushed the single button, which had an arrow pointing upward. Somewhere above her, she could hear the motor spring to life and the wheels begin to grind. She looked behind her again and saw Simon only a few feet away, still holding his stomach with one hand as he ran. The elevator would never get to her in time.

She sprinted for the stairs, using every last ounce of her energy to force her legs to move faster. Reaching the stairs ahead of Simon, she started up, taking two steps at a time. She was on the eighth step when he grabbed her right leg and pulled it out from under her. He jerked her roughly down the concrete stairs, spewing verbal abuse as her body was pounded into submission. She was forced to put her arms across her face to protect it, which left the rest of her body vulnerable to damage by the stairs and by Simon's flailing fists.

Back on the basement level, Simon dragged Mariele down the corridor, past the door to the morgue. She half expected to see Dwago come bursting through the door to confront Simon and resume their fight. It was hard to believe that the strong young man was dead. That was something Mariele never would have wished on him, no matter how much she hated him.

Dwago had stood up for her at the end of his life, trying to convince Simon to release her. Of course, Simon had no intention of letting her go. She had tried to escape, and he had caught her. Now, she only could wonder what he had planned for her. It was clear that he didn't care how much pain he caused her. All the feelings he once had for her seemed to have dissipated, or maybe they had been overcome by his own desperate need for survival.

Further down the corridor, Simon pushed Mariele through another door and down a dozen or so steps to a subterranean level. The air was thick and humid, and Mariele had trouble breathing immediately. Without being told, she knew that this was the lair of the graythings, the place where they dwelled while they were on the earth. It was the most frightening, ugly place she ever had seen.

It was almost inconceivable that just above them there was a hospital complex. In this underground hell, the walls dripped green slime into the putrid air, and there would be no relief from it unless she somehow found the steps again, and then found the energy to climb them. Already, Mariele doubted that she ever would leave this place. Even though she knew that her despair was part of the graythings' strategy for breaking her will, she couldn't resist giving in to it.

For the first time, she could picture how peaceful it would be to give in to them, and let her body be carried away once she was dead.

"Don't let yourself think that way," an inner voice told her, "because the graythings don't want your body now. They want your soul, and they will do everything within their power to get it."

"Well, how do you like your new home?" Simon asked, with a laugh that sounded more like a cackle than a human expression of mirth.

"Let go of me," Mariele demanded. "I want to go home, and I want to go now."

"I told you, you are home." More of the insane laughter issued from the vicinity of Simon's face, which Mariele could barely distinguish in the dim light.

He was still holding onto her, his hands, which she once had loved for their grace, clutching at her as if he might drown if he didn't hang on for dear life. They stood that way for a long time, in the underground chamber with its dripping walls and nauseating odors. When Simon started exhibiting signs of impatience and anxiety, sweating profusely and shifting nervously from one foot to another, it happened.

The air around them suddenly was filled with graythings. Mariele felt them touching her. They flapped around her head and Simon's, so many of them that there was no room for her to move away from them. There had been little air in the room; now, there was none. She thought that she would die of asphyxiation. The green slime was on her clothes and in her hair. She was gulping it in with every breath she took. Screams rose in her throat, but there was no air left to expel them.

When Simon spoke over the noise of the circling

creatures, they quieted and slowed their mad flapping.

"My gray masters, I came here to accuse you of taking my mother against her will." The graythings whipped against Mariele at breakneck speed in their attempts to surround Simon, but he wasn't finished. "I have relented. You were patient for many years, while my promises went unfulfilled. It is time I feed you and assuage your hunger. My mother was your appetizer. Now, you shall have your feast, a soul so pure that the angels will weep when you devour it."

The graythings grew more agitated, moving away from Simon, concentrating their attention on Mariele. They were so close that she could see the tiny red slits of their eyes staring at her. She was weakening, and it was very frightening. Would they use their damp bodies to suffocate her, or would they continue to drain off her energy, what they seemed to be doing now? Either way, she would be dead. There were so many of them that she surely wouldn't have to suffer long in this world.

But what of the next world? For all eternity, her soul would be separated from the soul of God. Simon had said they would "devour" her soul, and she wondered what pain she could suffer on earth that could compare with the pain of losing her soul?

With a sudden movement, she wrenched her arm free of Simon's grip, pushed him hard, and struck out at the graythings. They scattered, floating into each other, knocking against Simon. Seconds later, they were back, and Mariele was swiping at them with her arms again. Then, Simon was in front of her, grabbing ahold of her right arm and twisting it painfully behind her back.

"It's time to stop playing games, Mariele," he said, with a smirk. "As much as I love the game, I'm rapidly tiring of it. Now, we will get on with the business that brought us here."

She felt a prick on her right shoulder and looked down to see a fine red line of blood on her white skin. Then, she saw the scalpel which Simon had used to kill Dwago. He was holding it above her arm, as if he meant to demonstrate its power before he plunged it into her heart.

"For God's sake, get it over with," she pleaded. "If you mean to kill me, why torture me first?" The awful thought came to her as soon as she spoke those words: Maybe he did mean to torture her, to kill her slowly, with one small slice of the scalpel at a time.

"Simon, if you ever cared for me at all," she begged, "just kill me quickly, please."

He answered her plea with the same insane laughter that he had been exhibiting since they had arrived at the hospital.

"You really misunderstand the entire situation, Mariele. I'm not going to kill you. You're going to kill yourself."

"No, I won't."

"The graythings are waiting for you. Don't you

feel as if you almost can hear them? The excitement they must be feeling!"

"The damned things don't have feelings, Simon, what's the matter with you?"

"You'd better stop hurtling insults at them because soon you're going to belong to them. As soon as you plunge this scalpel into your chest, you'll feel your lifeblood flowing out of your veins, and you'll feel the graythings coming into you, becoming part of you. No, I said that wrong. You will become part of them, part of the eternity they share."

He tried to present the scalpel to her, obviously hoping that her desire to escape him was so great that she would decide to plunge the scalpel into her chest immediately. He was wrong. She hit his hand as hard as she could, and the sharp blade of the scalpel tore into his left shoulder. A fountain of blood spurted out, and Simon screamed in pain.

Mariele turned to run, but a few feet away from Simon, she was enclosed and surrounded by the graythings. They brushed against her, circling faster and faster, in a frenzy for the sacrifice Simon had promised them. As they pushed at her from all sides, she lost her balance, slid to the ground and stayed there, too exhausted to move.

The awful things exerted pressure on Mariele, physically and mentally. She gasped for air while they fluttered above her, and although the cavernous room was silent, she heard them chattering in her mind, even as she felt them nibbling at the corners of her consciousness.

She wondered if it was worth it to fight, since she had nothing left to live for anyway. Maybe, Simon was right. Maybe, the scalpel was the easy way out, the only way out. As thoughts of despair filled her mind, Simon appeared above her, the instrument of death extended in his hand. He smiled, not the unfamiliar sick smile he had been using today, but the one that had attracted her to him when she first had met him, in this very hospital.

Mariele reached up and took the scalpel from his hand, ignoring the graythings and their excited fluttering and flapping. She turned the scalpel toward her chest.

"Go on," Simon urged, in a soft voice. "Go on, do it."

It all made sense. Suddenly, it all made sense. She moved the scalpel toward her heart. It wouldn't take a hard thrust. It was so sharp . . . so wonderfully sharp. It would cut so deep, deep into her chest, deep into her heart. She closed her eyes, felt the scalpel prick the skin of her chest, then felt it being eased out of her hand.

"Get the hell away from her," Simon shouted. "She wants to do it, you have no right to interfere."

When she opened her eyes, the instant revulsion that she felt for the graythings was replaced by a wave of pity. The one who floated in front of her didn't look exactly like the others. He appeared to be in transition between the two worlds of the humans and the graythings. She imagined that she could see something of Ben's intense dark eyes in the way the thing looked at her.

"Ben?" she whispered. "Is that you, Ben?"

"They have no individuality," Simon answered her, "but whoever he is, that one will pay dearly for taking the scalpel away from you. They have no hands when the transition is complete, and he knows that he shouldn't be using his now." It all sounded so ridiculous that Mariele couldn't be sure whether Simon was joking or serious.

The thing moved toward Simon, but Simon stood up to it, and it whisked past him without harming him. As it passed, Simon reached out and made an attempt to grab the scalpel away from it. He couldn't get it, but he kept trying, slapping at the graything over and over again. Finally, on one of his tries, the sharp instrument, still in the possession of the graything, sliced into Simon's hand at the wrist. It cut easily through flesh and tendons and arteries, until it struck bone.

Simon screamed and held his right hand to his left armpit, in an attempt to staunch the flow of blood. There was more blood than Mariele ever had seen before. It flowed like a river from the bloody hand that dangled from the stump of his wrist. He started running around in circles, in imitation of the circling graythings. The faster he moved, the more blood poured from his arm. In what seemed like only a few minutes, he stopped running and dropped to the floor.

"Simon?" Mariele spoke his name into the silent room and begged him to answer. She had grown to be afraid of him today, but she didn't want him to die. And she didn't want to be alone with the graythings, even if one of them had tried to be kind to her and save her from Simon.

She moved toward his body slowly and cautiously, since she wasn't sure who had the scalpel now. She half expected him to jump up and attack her when she got close enough. But he didn't move. He just laid there in a widening puddle of blood with his eyes open, staring into nothingness.

Suddenly, Mariele was pushed backward by a great movement of air that felt like the flapping of a thousand giant pair of wings. The graythings came between her and Simon, and she was shoved away until her back was pressed up against the slimy wall of the cavern. The graythings lowered themselves to Simon's body, hovered, then rose up again to flutter near the ceiling high above her head. She lost track of the one who had taken the scalpel out of her hand, and now, she thought she might have imagined the whole thing.

One thing she was sure of, however, was that after several minutes, the graythings disappeared into thin air, leaving their den completely empty, except for her. They were gone, and so was Simon's body. She knew what had happened, or at least, she thought she did, and she thought that Simon probably would appreciate the irony of it. He had made so many promises to them, and each promise had been broken. Now, they had finally gotten him on a technicality. Although the graything had been holding the scalpel, it was Simon's own act that had killed him. He had thrust his wrist against the scalpel's blade and used it to make a mortal wound. Without the intention of committing suicide, he nearly had severed his hand and caused himself to bleed to death. He had fulfilled the suicide goddess's single criteria of self-destruction, and the graythings had accepted him as one of their own.